My name is Callum Ormond.
I am sixteen
and I am a hunted fugitive . . .

CONSPIRACY 365

BOOK TWELVE: DECEmBER

The cenotaph started to spin around me like I was trapped inside one of those anti-gravity carnival rides. Mum? Could Mum have been the person who – I tried to stop my brain from going there, but it was determined. If she was capable of turning her back on her son, could she also have been capable of . . . attacking me? Locking me in a coffin and leaving me to die underground?

Finally, Cal is within days of finding out the answers to all his questions . . . or dying in the attempt . . .

here. I'm so close to confronting Sligo, but I know I shouldn't do it. Not yet. Not without you. Oh, Cal, where are you? I really need you right now. I don't know what to do. I need you to talk sense into me. Please call.'

Beep.

'I don't know why I can't stop crying—I always suspected it. I always knew in my heart Sligo must have murdered them. I've made my decision and I'm on my way over to see him now. I've been waiting for six years to find out the truth, this can't wait another second.'

She'd always been there for me, and the one time she needed me, I'd ignored her.

I lifted her up and shook her gently.

My phone suddenly vibrated in my pocket, reminding me again of the unheard voicemail messages. I knelt up to get a better hold of Winter and my mobile tumbled out of my pocket and hit the floor of the container.

The bump had activated the loudspeaker function.

'You have four new messages,' said the voice on my phone.

After a beep, Winter's recorded voice reverberated ominously through the container as I held her lifeless body in my arms.

'Cal, it's me. I'm at the car yard and I have amazing news! I just found Mum and Dad's car and got inside. It's our car, that's for sure—I found the tiny bird I had drawn on the upholstery in the back when I was nine! I *knew* it was here. I knew it! Call me back!'

Beep.

'Me again. Please call me back when you get this message. I checked the car over . . . and I was right. The brake lines had been cut . . . Cal, Sligo did it. He murdered my parents.'

Beep.

'Cal, where are you?! I feel like I'm going crazy

by the burnout of a car speeding away.

Griff groaned beside me, half leaning against the container wall. On my knees, I crawled around in the darkness, reaching out blindly, feeling for Winter.

'Winter? Are you in here?' I called.

My frantic searching continued, moving carefully along the hard, cold floor of the metal container. Griff joined me.

'Winter?' I called again.

'Cal!' Griff croaked. 'There's someone else in here! I think I just felt a leg!'

I scrambled to Griff's side, feeling around him. 'She's just here,' said Griff. 'I think she's dead!'

'Winter? Winter?' I shouted, finally feeling her wild hair, and finding her face. 'Can you hear me?' I asked, holding her up.

There was no answer. She was cold.

'Winter?' I cried. 'Winter? Please talk to me!'

I grabbed her hands and squeezed them.

Cold.

I put my head down on her chest, trying to hear a heartbeat, desperate to find a pulse in her neck.

Cold.

All I could hear was Griff Kirby whimpering and the sound of my fearful heart.

I was too late.

to Zombie Two, then hauled Griff over to the container and pushed him inside. I heard Griff grunt as he fell to the floor.

'What have you done to Winter?' I pleaded. 'Where is she?'

The two thugs ignored me. Instead of answering me, Zombie Two lifted me up, and wrenched my arms into position behind my back. But instead of restraining my hands, he just kicked me, sending me stumbling into the container.

I struggled to my feet and charged towards the opening. 'What have you done with Winter?' I screeched, before being knocked back down again, this time by Bruno.

'Just shut up and you won't get hurt,' he said, 'for now. The boss will be opening a bottle of French champagne when I tell him what we've just caught! We've been trying to take you out of the picture for months, and now you've just handed yourself over. You practically begged to be thrown into the container. It's too easy. Like trapping rabbits!'

'Let us out!' cried Griff.

'Not going to happen,' said Bruno. 'I guess this is goodbye.'

Hearing the container doors slamming shut was horrendous. Then came the awful sound of the locking device clicking into place, followed

Whack! The rock clanged loudly on the metal wall of the container.

Griff froze, but it was too late.

'Who's there?' came Zombie Two's snarling voice. 'Who's that?'

I jumped down the stairs and hauled Griff up. 'On your feet! Quick!'

It was too late. Bruno suddenly materialised from nowhere, and Zombie Two loomed up behind us.

'You! This time I finish you!' Zombie Two shouted.

He pounced on me, almost breaking my arm as he threw me to the ground.

I lay squashed on my stomach, his heavy boot pressed on the small of my back, my arm painfully twisted back in his gorilla grip.

'Make move, and is last move you make! Understood?'

'Understood,' I gasped.

I turned my head to see Griff Kirby pinned to the ground under Bruno's knee. Now Bruno was talking on the phone.

'Gotcha, boss,' he said.

Bruno put away his phone and pulled out a large roll of electrical tape from his pocket. He wrapped Griff's wrists behind him before dragging him to his feet. He threw the roll of tape the container being opened or closed. That meant Zombie Two, Bruno or even Sligo himself could be close by. I couldn't see any light down there.

Suddenly I heard a voice. Someone was speaking near the container. I strained to listen.

'OK, boss.' It was the voice of Zombie Two! 'I about to lock it,' he said in his thick accent, 'then she ready to go.'

Did he mean the container was ready to go, or did 'she' mean Winter? A horrifying thought came to me. Winter was in the container! Bound for who-knows-where!

'She's in the container!' I mouthed to Griff. Winter was in there and Zombie Two was about to lock it up!

But why wasn't Winter yelling and banging on the walls, demanding to be let out? The container was just metres from us. Why was she so silent?

Fear was spreading rapidly through my body. 'We have to get her out!' I whispered. 'Before he locks the container! Come on!'

Griff looked petrified, but in what must have been a sudden burst of bravery he stood up from where we'd been squatting and leaped down the stairs. He landed awkwardly, then tripped over something, kicking a rock up at the side of the container.

there? Was Sligo importing car parts? Or was it loaded with machinery for export?

It was dark, but beyond the bulk of the container and the truck, I saw a light in the office where I first encountered Vulkan Sligo. Was Winter sitting in that same chair, with her hands taped tightly, being interrogated, like I had been?

If it hadn't been for her that day, I would have drowned in the oil tank. She'd saved me. And we were strangers back then.

'Follow me,' I whispered to Griff, and moved forward.

'Someone's in there!' Griff hissed in my ear.

'Winter might be in there,' I hissed back.

'I think we should get out of here.'

'If you're too scared to help,' I growled, 'just go. Get out of here.'

'I may be scared,' said Griff, 'but I'm not leaving without you.'

We crept up the stairs towards the office, but as we made our way to the door the clang of metal behind us made me swing around. I ducked and pulled Griff down with me.

'What was that?' Griff whispered in my ear.

'No idea. Let's go down and take a look.'

We retraced our footsteps down the stairs. The sound I'd heard could have been the doors of

'Where are we?' he asked again.

'Vulkan Sligo's car yard.'

Griff swore and stopped in his tracks, clearly terrified.

'Come on!' I hissed, as I darted across the road and hurled myself at the cyclone fence. I searched frantically for a sign of Zombie Two, Bruno, Sligo and, of course, Winter. All seemed quiet.

I threw my backpack down on the other side of the fence, and using my hoodie to protect my hands from the barbed wire, was able to haul myself over and down. Griff grunted as he mimicked my movements.

I looked left and right, fearing we'd be picked up on security cameras or that automatic lights would flood the area, highlighting our presence.

With Griff behind me, I set off, keeping low and as close as possible to the piles of car bodies. A stray cat screeched, making my hair stand on end. I'd almost trodden on her. She bounded away, disappearing back into blackness.

'I can't see where I'm going,' grizzled Griff.

Bent over, we continued our hobbling run between the piles of cars until we'd come to the open area in front of the office block. I pulled up short. A huge container stood on the back of a truck, parked out the front. What was it doing looked at me in horror. Now it was his turn to shake me. 'Don't just stand there, Cal, say something!'

For the moment, all thoughts of the DMO, and our seemingly impossible escape to Ireland, were driven from my mind. All I could think of was my friend Winter and how to find her.

'They're taking her somewhere,' I said. 'Loading her up.'

'Loading her up . . . in what?'

'I don't know,' I said, wishing like crazy Boges was here to help. 'But there's no time to waste. Let's go!'

Car yard

9:30 pm

We ran through the dark without speaking. I hung a right-hand turn, heading towards Sligo's car yard. Griff was just a few metres behind me. That was where he'd lock her up, I figured. The yard seemed to be where he, or his thugs, carried out all of his dirty work. I just hoped she was OK, and that Sligo simply wanted her out of his life, not her life to be over.

'Where are we?' Griff asked, running towards me.

I didn't answer.

the way up to Carnegie Street, the whole time trying to fight off thoughts of what could be happening to Winter.

7:36 pm

The sight of Winter's bag lying in the gutter, filthy from being run over, sent horrifying chills up my spine. The contents of her bag were strewn over the bitumen, and I automatically started picking them up. A squashed hairbrush, some lip gloss, a crushed pen. Griff started helping me. I grabbed her bag and pulled it open. Miraculously, her mobile was unharmed, inside. As I checked it over, it rang.

I pressed 'answer', but didn't say anything. I simply waited.

'Well, well, well, Winter Frey,' Sligo's voice bellowed down the line. 'My *sham* daughter. My little *spy*. You will pay for what you've done to me! After everything I've done for you. Everything I've given you! Taken you under my wing! This is how you repay me? Ha! Bruno and Zombrovski will be loading you up and sending you away so that I never have to see your pitiful orphan face ever again!' he shouted. 'If only the accident—when *Daddy* "lost control"—had taken you, too,' he said with a wicked laugh. 'Goodbye!'

Sligo hung up and I was left speechless. Griff

'You saw *what* happen?' I said, shaking him. 'What's happened to her? *Where is she?*'

He wriggled out of my grasp and I let him go, all my energy focused on his words. 'She was just snatched off the street! I saw the whole thing! They dragged her into a car, kicking and screaming! I raced after the car but it was no use.'

The desperation and the fear in his face must have been a mirror of my own. The chill in my heart dropped to sub zero.

'What car? Who grabbed her?'

'She was dragged into a black Subaru. I got part of the registration number. I couldn't do anything to save her! All her stuff's scattered over the road!'

The black Subaru. *Sligo.* Everything around me started spinning. If Sligo had discovered that she was a spy, under his nose, and that she had taken his scram money from him . . . or if he'd found her searching his car yard . . . or if he'd found out about me . . . I had to block it all out of my mind and concentrate. Every minute was crucial to saving her.

'What are we going to do?' Griff was pleading.

'I'm thinking, I'm *thinking*! Take me to where it happened.'

Without another word, Griff turned and ran, heading away from the beach. I ran with him all answer your phone now? angry at me? payback?

Something caught my attention up high, and I glanced up above the rocks to see a figure waving on the top of the cliff. I stood up and squinted my eyes.

It wasn't Winter, it was a guy. A guy who was waving and yelling and running down towards me.

I jumped down from the rock and prepared to take off. I didn't have time to deal with this right now. I couldn't risk waiting around any longer.

'Cal! I have to talk to you!'

I blinked at the approaching figure. It was Griff Kirby racing towards me—his red hair unmistakeable. I started running. There was no way this guy was going to set me up again!

'No! Don't run off like that! You have to help! Winter is in serious trouble!'

At the mention of her name, I skidded to a halt and turned around.

'What would you know?' I asked him.

'She's in trouble,' he said again. He was doubled over, trying to catch his breath.

I charged over to him, grabbing him by the shoulders. 'You already said that. Why are *you* telling me?'

'I saw it happen! She yelled out to me, "Find Cal! Tell him what's happened! Try the beach!"'

3:45 pm

I was still feeling dazed from my conversation with my uncle when my phone started beeping again—reminding me I had voicemail messages to check. I also had four text messages from Winter, from last night and this morning.

I stretched my legs out on the bench, and began reading.

📱 cal! call me back!

📱 what's going on? please call me back! I have more HUGE news!

📱 u ok? how come you're not answering? i've left you a million voicemail messages!

📱 PLEASE answer your phone. seriously going crazy here. i need u. can u meet me at the beach today?

Immediately I dialled her phone, but there was no answer. Three times.

I didn't know what else to do but to head straight to the beach.

6:40 pm

Waiting near the rocks, I scanned the horizon for any sign of Winter. A couple of hours had passed already and I was starting to get impatient. I decided to text her.

📱 at the beach. still waiting for u. why won't u

Ormond Singularity. You're safest in hiding, or behind bars, believe me.'

As much as I hated what he was saying, his words made sense to me. The bad guys had tracked me down easily when I was at home. They'd tracked me down when I was with my other family members, like Great-uncle Bartholomew and Great-aunt Millicent.

'So is it true?' Rafe asked.

'Is what true?'

'Samuel? He's alive? Please don't say so unless you've seen him in the flesh for yourself. Have you?'

'He's alive. I have seen him.'

Rafe let out a strange gulping sound, like he was trying to hold back tears.

'Every day,' he said, 'I have prayed it would happen.'

'Does Mum know anything about Dad's discovery?' I asked, quickly.

'She's so fragile, Cal,' said Rafe, slowly. 'I've done everything possible to keep it from her. It'd be far too risky if she got involved. But in another month, the danger will be over. Then I can explain everything to her. Then you can come home and together we'll clear your name and get our lives back. I promise.'

'But you did the opposite. You turned your back on me. And why would I want to shoot my uncle? What reason did you tell yourself?'

'Look, Cal, I understand you now know about Samuel.'

'What does he have to do with it?'

'The abduction damaged the family in ways you cannot imagine. We were so lucky to find you again, but no-one really knew what had happened to you. Or what the kidnappers had put you through. Hours had passed between the time you went missing and the time you were found. I guess we were always hoping you'd turn out OK, but we feared there'd be scars that would surface later in life.'

'And that one day I'd go on a shooting rampage and try to kill my family?'

'Cal,' he said, like he was shaking his head. 'One can never predict how the mind will cope with trauma.'

'So you figured I'd flipped out, from being abandoned as a child, then you go ahead and let history repeat itself.'

'Can't you see that you've been safer on the run? I know it hasn't been easy, but if you were here with us, you'd be like a sitting duck. The people we are up against are implacable—they will stop at nothing. You are the heir to the want you worrying about those drawings. Tom told me about his discovery in Ireland . . . and how dangerous it was. The more I learned about it, the more I realised the extent of the danger you were in.'

'I don't understand,' I said.

I was shocked. Rafe knew about everything?

'Are you serious? You've known about this all along? Why haven't you helped me? I've been out on my own for eleven months! I've been fighting for my life, my freedom, my sanity! And you could have helped me! Why did you tell the police I shot you? Why did you tell them I attacked my sister? Why would you do that?'

'Take it easy, Cal. Just hear me out. I didn't lie about the attack in Richmond. At the time I believed you shot me.'

'At the time? Does that mean you don't think that any more?'

'I don't know. I was never one hundred per cent certain, but then the police found your fingerprints on my gun.'

'Haven't we been over this before? I touched the gun at your house when I was looking for the drawings. What did you have the gun for anyway?'

'Because I wanted to protect you. I knew danger was brewing.'

'I've only ever wanted to protect my family,' I said, for what felt like the billionth time.

'I also wanted to speak to you about . . . my behaviour, earlier this year. I seem to have lost touch with people as I've grown older. Especially with young people. I don't want you to make any mistakes about me. Or where I'm coming from.'

'I'm listening.'

He took a deep breath and I waited for him to continue.

'I felt very responsible, Cal, after your dad was . . . was no longer with us. I felt it was my responsibility to look after my brother's family. You guys. I wanted to take it all on myself—not just the matters relating to the estate, but every-thing. I didn't want any of you suffering any more. Especially your mother. She's experienced far too much tragedy for one person.'

Automatically I started reading into his words. He didn't want us suffering any more? Did he mean after the abduction?

'I realise now that I was foolish to think I could handle it alone. I should have included you more—after all, you turned sixteen this year. We should have been allies.'

'What about the package—' I began to say, but he continued.

'I intercepted that package because I didn't

I wasn't sure about speaking to Rafe, but I figured I had nothing to lose by ringing him. Seeing the newspaper clipping of his bizarre interview after the abduction had turned him into even more of a mystery to me.

'Hello, Rafe speaking,' he answered on the third ring.

'It's Cal.'

'I was hoping you'd call,' he said, sounding sincerely pleased. 'Thank you.'

'What did you want to talk about?'

'This is long overdue, I think. I—' Rafe sounded nervous. He had never been much of a talker, so I knew this wasn't going to be easy for him. Whatever it was. 'I saw you stop the sniper at the chapel,' he said. 'I know you saved me from a bullet. The cops might think otherwise, but I know what I saw, and I saw my nephew coming to my rescue.'

'Have you told the cops that?'

'Of course. However, they were unconvinced. So many of the guests claimed that you were the one with the weapon. Too many. They denied seeing another armed man. I was the only witness who claimed otherwise.'

'What about Mum? Or Gabbi?'

'They didn't see anything, I'm afraid,' he said. 'So, thank you, Cal.'

30 NOVEMBER

32 days to go . . .

Treehouse

12:58 pm

I went to check my messages and missed calls, but was interrupted by an incoming call from Boges.

'Cal, I only have a second to talk, but I just wanted to tell you that your uncle really wants to speak to you. Can you call him?'

'What about?'

'I have to go, sorry.'

'Didn't you see me on the news last night? I was at the big game,' I joked.

'Dude, you're always on TV.' I could hear the school buzzer going off in the background. 'Call you later,' said Boges, before abruptly hanging up.

That was weird, I thought to myself, but Boges was probably just busy and being cautious about contacting me after his run-in with the cops.

I climbed out of the suit and grabbed my back-pack off the wall. I hoped the visiting team didn't mind me pinching a jersey, scarf and beanie, but I had to do whatever I could to get out.

With the beanie jammed down over my ears, and the scarf swinging over my jersey, I shoved my hands in my pockets and ambled past the security guards who were supposed to be guarding the changing room wings. It was surprisingly easy to do, because they were both glued to the television monitor, on the wall, broadcasting the game.

On my right, a group of cops were huddled round a couple of guys about my age, demanding identification. On my left were two cops, watching the entrance. I spotted half a hotdog in a rubbish bin nearby, and quickly picked it up. I took a big, convincing bite out of it as I strolled past them.

As soon as I made it out of the stadium and saw that I was in the clear, I spat out the gross, cold mouthful of hotdog, and grinned.

I'd made it out.

The policewoman swiftly left the room and rejoined her partner. The voices slowly receded. The last remark I could hear was, 'I told you so.'

At those words, I slumped with relief, still shaking.

The voices had faded and the thumping boots moved away. I'd been *saved* by the cop in charge.

Or so I thought.

Footsteps approached once more.

Again, I turned to stone. Surely my luck had run out.

'Nothing in here,' called a voice. 'Apart from a koala bear.'

'Koala's aren't *bears*,' someone corrected him.

'So what are they? Sure looks like a bear to me.'

Please, take your stupid argument elsewhere, I silently begged.

6:16 pm

Finally, they left and everything was quiet. I was sweating, drenched inside the koala suit. A long time passed before I dared to move.

I lifted off the koala head, and sucked in some fresh air.

The rumble from the crowd started returning, like they'd decided to carry on with the game, in spite of the disruption—me. That meant I had until half-time to get out of here.

'Shower area clear. No-one here.'

I almost slumped further with relief as the officer left the room.

'Hey, check out that koala mascot!' called the woman who had shouted out orders earlier. 'I always wanted to wear one of those things.'

'Grow up!' the guy said, mockingly. 'Have you secured the rest of the corridor?'

'No, seriously,' she persisted. 'I'm going to try it on. Send someone else in and I'll give them a fright!'

My body was shaking uncontrollably now. I shut my eyes tight, trying to decide what to do. Should I jump up and scare them? Take advantage of their surprise to gain a few seconds?

'You're not serious,' said the other cop. 'C'mon. Grow up. The boss won't be impressed.'

Please, I willed her, *listen to him!*

All I could see was the dark blue fabric of the woman's police overalls blocking what little vision I had. Any minute now, she'd grab the headpiece. I readied myself to move suddenly and swiftly. Her arms reached out to lift it.

'What the hell do you think you're doing?' spat a stern voice. 'You're supposed to be searching for a dangerous psychopath, not playing dress-ups!'

My heart stopped.

'Yes, Sergeant!'

up on a nearby hook, where it blended in with all the other bags, grabbed the koala suit, shoved my legs into it, pulled my arms through the grey sleeves, and with hands made clumsy by the padded paw gloves, I grabbed the huge headpiece, and thrust it over my head.

The koala mascot suit was huge on me. I collapsed my knees and hung my head limply, so that the costume looked lifeless and empty again.

Then I froze.

Maybe, just maybe, I could fool them. In the position I was in, I could just see out with one eye, through a mesh section in the head.

I held my breath when I heard a voice. If I could have, I would have stopped my heart beating just for those few moments. To me it sounded like it was almost thumping louder than the roars of the crowds outside.

'Another changing room,' a voice called. 'I'll check it.'

Footsteps approached. I saw part of the guy's uniform. I was like a statue as he walked past me, not daring to breathe.

The footsteps moved away.

'Check the showers!' a woman shouted out.

I heard the swing of the shower doors, as the cubicles were checked.

police calling each other as they searched and cleared the rooms behind me.

It was only a matter of time before they reached this room.

I could still hear the muted roars of the crowd in the stadium above me: 'We want Cal! We want Cal!'

It was a frenzy!

My heart was racing, my brain feverish with useless ideas on how to escape. I grabbed a football jersey and started pulling it on. Who are you kidding? I asked myself, as I caught my reflection in a mirror. I looked like wanted fugitive, Cal Ormond, now wearing a football jersey. I threw the jersey to the ground, cursing at the crooked stare of the sightless koala mascot.

A huge riot cop stormed into the room opposite.

After everything I'd gone through, and within days of organising flights out of the country, I was trapped under a stadium.

The heavy boots of the approaching police officers stomped closer. Any second now, they'd spring me. Hopelessly, I scanned the room again for a place to hide, beyond the bench with the clothes and over to the koala mascot. Its black plastic eyes seemed to stare crookedly into mine.

My hiding place was staring straight at me!

I dived over to the bench, hurled my backpack

I dodged cheerleaders and a goofy-looking mascot, and was running back down the ramp where I'd entered the grounds. I had no option but to keep going, even though I knew it led underneath the stadium and not out of it. There was no alternative. I avoided one final tackle from a player who went skidding into the hoardings around the edge of the oval, much to the delight of the noisy bystanders, and then I darted down the ramp again, disappearing from the cameras, and public view.

It was quieter down here but I knew I only had a few moments before someone would catch me. I raced along the network of corridors with various rooms and dressing rooms off them, trying to find a way out. Already, I could hear the yelling and shouting of the police and their pounding footsteps.

I took a chance and ran into one of the rooms at the end of the tunnel—obviously a dressing room—with showers at one end and a row of benches around the walls, littered with jerseys, boots and towels. There was a window, but it was high up in the wall, barred and locked, offering no escape.

A huge koala mascot costume leaned lopsidedly against a wall at the end of the benches.

Outside in the corridors, I could hear the

were providing a new game—Chase the Fugitive—and the crowd was loving it. They were all pointing at me like I was a horse at the races.

I couldn't avoid seeing myself up there on the screen as I moved this way then that, sprinting in zigzag angles, confusing the football players who were trying to catch me.

I'd almost forgotten about Pepper Cop—I was just running! Players came at me from all angles but I was smaller and faster. I'd had almost a year's training now and I wasn't just here to win a match, I was running for my life!

I ducked and swerved, avoiding them, while the crowd was chanting, 'Cal-lum, Cal-lum, Cal-lum!'

A stream of police officers poured onto the ground, and now a siren was wailing over the top of the chanting. In the grandstands, the crowd started booing the police! The angry mob was whistling and hissing at them, like the police were the opponents!

For some strange reason the crowd was on my side! It didn't make sense! I was the Psycho Kid, not their *hero*!

The masses in the stands were now shouting, 'Go Cal! Go Cal!' It spurred me on, and I exploded in one direction then, swivelling like an ice-skater, I skidded away in the completely opposite direction, and out of the stadium.

the tens of thousands of fans who seethed with hysterical excitement for the upcoming match and their team.

Players from the opposing team stormed onto the oval, and the home crowd exploded into menacing booing and hissing. I looked around me—huge spotlights shone down like a hundred police choppers. I was a fugitive, mixed up in the beginning of a highly anticipated football match!

My eyes darted around, searching for an escape, running over the crowd like a Mexican wave. Another tremendous roar erupted—even louder and more intimidating than before. My sight stopped circling. I'd landed on the massive television screen, looming high on one end of the stadium. On it was a huge close-up of me!

My face!

I'd been recognised! Again the crowd roared like thunder. I ducked and ran but was immediately tackled down by one of the players who'd spotted the impostor. The audience went wild! Winded, I struggled to my feet. Now the crowd was yelling out my name!

'Cal-lum! Cal-lum! Cal-lum! Cal-lum!'

I took off, running, as fast as my legs would carry me. I had to go faster than ever—I had professional sportsmen on my tail. The sound from the crowd was insane! The TV cameramen gates of the stadium, pouring into the grand-stand. I fought my way clear of the group, only to be caught up again in another.

Over the commotion of the rowdy football fans, attendants were yelling about tickets.

I wondered where my pursuer was.

I ducked under some scaffolding and found myself on a ramp where the footballers them-selves suddenly appeared, charging up the slope, pumped to the max, about to hurl themselves onto the field. But it wasn't only the players who suddenly appeared: alongside them was Pepper Spray Cop!

Somehow he'd managed to keep me in sight. He was bearing down on me, pushing his way past people to get closer. He looked more deter-mined than ever to get me.

'Hey!' he shouted, as I ducked into the line of players. They were so fired up and focused that they didn't even notice me as they surged along.

Before I knew it, I was running out onto the oval with them! I ducked behind one of the play-ers as I ran into the stadium, barely conscious of the exposure of my surroundings, desperate to escape the vengeful cop and the rest of the police backup he'd have behind him.

I was dimly aware of the roar going up from

My phone vibrated—it was Winter calling again. Suddenly I felt eyes on my back. Someone was watching me again, I was sure of it.

I increased my pace, and the warning bells in my head increased too.

Someone was watching me from a car, lingering on my right.

I tensed up as I turned to see who my quiet observer was. I couldn't believe my rotten luck.

Of all the cops in the city conducting crowd control, it had to be him—Pepper Spray Cop! The guy I'd escaped from months ago!

He saw the shock in my face, and his suspicions were confirmed.

He was on to me. As he scrambled to jump out of the car, I ran.

I shoved and jostled my way through the crowds, ignoring the angry shouts of the people I was barrelling through. I didn't have time to apologise—my freedom was at stake!

I pushed and squeezed my way into the masses, forcing through, hoping that it would be impossible for him or any other cop to find me in this huge throng.

Ten minutes later, I found myself being carried along by this great wave of sports fans. It was out of control. *I* was being pushed now, and realised I was being hauled through the open

I could feel my phone vibrating on silent in my pocket, and when I saw that it was Boges calling, I hit 'answer' as fast as possible. I ducked into an alley to take the call.

'Boges! What happened? Are you OK?'

'Man, they drilled me. It was a tough few hours. They wanted to know everything, but don't worry, I don't think I've done any damage. I impressed myself with how good I am at lying now. I've become a master. Sometimes I remember the lies better than I remember the truth.'

'I know what you mean,' I admitted. 'Thanks, Boges. I'm so sorry you had to—'

The phone cut out. I almost threw it on the ground in frustration—the signal had dropped out. I'd have to try him later.

5:20 pm

I was walking towards the football stadium. Crowds of people in the red and white colours of the local team were gathering ahead of me. It looked like they'd just piled off some buses at the bay. I wished I had my own red and white gear so I could lose myself among them all.

The crowds were building up fast, and I noticed more and more cops and security guards milling around. I'd have to take the long way home to avoid them.

answered the phone. That made him laugh. He said he couldn't think of anything better on the spot.

I filled him in on the Boges situation, and he told me he'd do anything he could to help. He also said he'd look into December flights to Ireland for us.

'I'll see what I can find out about Boges,' said Sharkey. 'If I can help him, I will. I have to go now. The big game starts soon, and I have to get my couch ready!'

I was so out of the loop, I had no idea what game he was even talking about. And I'd forgotten to ask him about how his hot date went, the night Winter broke into Sligo's scram bag. I knew Sharkey wasn't going to offer up that information without a fair amount of pestering.

4:40 pm

My phone started beeping; I had a voicemail message from Winter. She must have called again while I was on the phone to Sharkey. I didn't bother listening to it, dialling her number instead.

Just before it began ringing, a squad car cruised past and I was forced to hang up and shove my phone back in my pocket, pull my collar up and my cap down, and walk on. Eric Blair and Nelson Sharkey were right. Strike Force Predator had intensified.

'Thanks, Detective,' I said. 'I tried telling them they had the wrong person. They thought I was that fugitive kid, Callum Ormond. They wouldn't believe me when I said it wasn't me!'

The two cops released me from their grip, and shamefully hung their heads.

'Come on, Matt,' said Nelson, yanking my arm.

Once we were a few metres away, he whispered to me. 'We'd better go our separate ways now. Stay focused. The police hunt for you has intensified. Strike Force Predator has doubled in size. They've promised the public that you'll be behind bars before the year is out. You have the passport—that was the reason I called the meeting so take it away and get out of here. You can thank me later.'

And with that, he darted across the road and out of sight.

Guilt sat in my chest like heartburn. I'd thought for a second that Sharkey had betrayed me, and then he'd come to my rescue, yet again.

The pressure was on. It seemed like everyone was working to the 31 December deadline. I had the passport, now we just needed to book flights . . . and get Boges out of the limelight.

After a few minutes of walking, I quickly rang Sharkey to thank him for saving me again.

'Hi, Detective Dane Cooper,' I said when he

who the heck are you?' the cop demanded with a sneer.

'He's Matt Marlow, that's who,' came a familiar voice, loud and commanding.

I managed to twist around to see Nelson Sharkey approaching. He rushed to my side and swiftly produced something, seemingly from my back pocket.

'You have the wrong kid, officers,' he said, waving a small book in his hand. He flipped through its pages. 'This is certainly not Callum Ormond. Take a look for yourselves,' he said, handing it to them.

It was my new passport! Unbelievably, and in the nick of time, it had finally arrived!

'Don't make fools of yourselves and the police force,' continued Sharkey. 'You can't arrest kids like this without even checking their ID. Senior Sergeant McGrath would not be happy about this. He can't stand it when the rookies on his shift mess up.'

The cops squirmed uncomfortably.

'And who are you?' one of them asked.

'Detective Dane Cooper,' he lied, 'from Clarendale. You'd better let this kid go before I report you two turkeys. I could hit you both with a false imprisonment charge, or detaining a minor without a supervising adult present.'

I strained my head up to see. Black police boots scuffed the footpath near my face.

My hands were wrenched behind my back and secured.

Eric's warning about the airport security suddenly hit me. He'd said someone had started a rumour about me fleeing the country. I had no idea who that person could have been . . . until now.

Sharkey had set me up. I took a breath and tried not to throw up.

'You sure this is the kid? He doesn't look like this in the poster,' said a voice behind me, as I was jerked to my feet.

'It's him, all right. They never look like the poster.' Two plain-clothes police officers grasped me on both sides. I had no chance of escape.

'Let me go! What have I done wrong?'

'You're Callum Ormond. We've been after you for nearly a year,' said one cop. 'Just wait till the boss hears *we're* hauling him in!' he said to his partner.

'*I'm* not Callum Ormond!' I scoffed. They started dragging me off the street and towards an unmarked car. I couldn't let them take me to a station. If they fingerprinted me, I'd be dead. 'You have the wrong guy!'

'Yeah, well if you ain't Callum Ormond, then

council meeting so i went back to the car yard . . . i just found what i was looking for in my parents' car! now i have proof it's theirs! call me asap!

I was about to call her back when a deep uneasiness squirmed through me. I was becoming an expert at knowing when something was wrong.

I noticed a guy standing about a hundred metres from the gym, eyeing me. He quickly looked away as if he'd realised I'd spotted him staring. There was another guy looking at me suspiciously, from the other side of the street.

Was I under surveillance?

I started hurrying back the way I'd come when I thought I saw a woman talking into her collar. I swung back. The two men I'd seen before were no longer there.

Without warning, someone crash-tackled me to the ground. I fell heavily.

The side of my face and my right hand grated painfully along the ground. I tried rolling over but the heavy body on top of me pinned me to the ground.

'Get off me! Who are you?' I shouted. 'What do you think you're doing?'

'Police! Stay right where you are! Stay on the ground! Don't move!'

criminals. That didn't worry me. Boges was smarter than all of them combined.

'Cal, when all of this is over—' Winter said, dismally looking around the treehouse before jumping to the ground. 'I think we should—'

She stopped abruptly.

'What?' I asked.

'Another time,' she said. 'I'd better go.'

I watched her through the gaps in the leaves as she snuck over the Lovetts' back fence, wondering what it was she had wanted to say.

As Winter vanished, I suddenly felt very alone. I couldn't do anything to help my friend, after he'd done nothing but help me throughout this whole year.

3:10 pm

A message beeped on my mobile and I dived for it. For once I was disappointed it was Sharkey.

📱 meet me at the gym in an hour.

3:16 pm

I headed for the gym, striding fast, glad to have a distraction.

In less than an hour, I was almost there. I was just a couple of streets away when my mobile beeped again.

📱 cal! been trying to call u! sligo had to go to a

We waited and the moment passed, the chopper moving away towards the city.

She turned back to me. 'Sligo has been watching me like a hawk—it's getting worse. He's always wanting to know where I am—what I'm doing. It's making it impossible for me to get back to the car yard. He thinks I'm at the flat right now but if he drops round and realises I'm not there, I'll be grilled with questions. I'm convinced he's suspicious of me. I'm scared he'll notice his scram money is missing and know I had something to do with it.'

'Why would he think that?'

'I don't know, but I'm freaking out. I have to go. I have to get back to the flat.'

'What should we do about Boges?'

'I don't know! I'm too afraid to call him right now. You shouldn't call him either—the cops might zero in on where you're hiding if you try. I'll find out what I can and call you back. OK?'

'OK,' I said, even though it wasn't OK. I hated the thought of Boges being pushed around by the police simply because he was my friend. But I knew he would never betray me, even though Winter had a point—they might trick him or manipulate him in some way. They were experts in extracting information, even from the toughest pressure him. Even charge him with being an accessory to your crimes.'

'They couldn't do that!'

'Can you imagine what that would do to his mum and his old granny? If Boges goes into juvenile detention? If they threaten to charge him with some criminal offence, he can kiss his future goodbye. They could make his life plan totally disappear. Everything he's ever dreamed of down the toilet.'

I started pacing in the tight space. She was right. I recalled the conversation with Toecutter Durham, about how lives can be destroyed with just one mistake.

'Cal, we have to do something!'

I had to think of a plan to get him out of trouble, while staying out of trouble myself. The only chance I had of discovering the truth about the Ormond Singularity waited for me in Ireland. I couldn't be caught at this stage.

Overhead I heard the sound that I'd come to dread—the chopping reverberations of a helicopter.

Winter saw my fear. Without a word, she poked her head out of the window and peered through the leaves.

'It's the police,' she said. 'Let's hope it's just flying over.'

about failure. I wouldn't fail. I *couldn't* fail.

I was looking through my notes, drawings and photos, spread out on the cramped floor of the treehouse, when I heard her voice outside.

'Cal? You there?'

Winter's voice was urgent, scared.

I stopped what I was doing.

'What is it?'

'Quickly. Toss me the rope!'

I let it down and she climbed up, squirming through the back window, almost losing the ribbon that was around her hair in the process.

As soon as I saw her face I knew something was wrong.

'It's Boges,' she said, almost in tears. 'The cops have Boges.'

'What? Have they arrested him?'

'I don't know, but they've taken him in for questioning. He slipped a split-second call through to me. He couldn't get through to you. They've been questioning him for hours. I was at Sligo's when he called, so I couldn't come straight over. Cal, I'm really worried. I'm scared that Boges will say where you're hiding!'

'Boges would never do that,' I said, checking my mobile for service. 'He'd never give me up. He would never betray me.'

'You don't know how hard the cops could

29 NOVEMBER

33 days to go . . .

Treehouse

10:00 am

The last few days had been tough. With the new police initiative, cops were literally everywhere. Boges warned me to keep a low profile until my passport was ready. The thought of Rathbone in Ireland was a constant worry. What was he up to? What was he discovering?

Every day I called Nelson Sharkey with the same question: 'Is my passport ready?' And every day I got the same answer: 'I told you, I'll let you know when it is.'

Midnight on the 31st of December—when the Ormond Singularity ran out—came closer and closer, like *it* was chasing me too. I only had *a few weeks left*! I'd survived, so far, like I'd been told to do, but I hadn't exposed the DMO. I hadn't cleared my name. I hadn't fulfilled my promise to Dad. I couldn't bring myself to think

'Of course it's probably nothing more than a rumour,' said Eric. 'Who knows how these things start.'

Every instinct told me it wasn't just a rumour. I thanked Eric, said goodbye and hurried out.

kidnapping, and now being wanted for crimes I didn't commit. Was there a connection between the two?

'I could help you,' offered Eric. 'Help you make a new life somewhere, interstate. A new identity, a job. I know a few people who might be helpful. At least you'd be safer under a new name.'

I shook my head. 'Thanks, but no, I still have too much to do.'

I wanted my life back, not a *new* life.

He reached for his wallet and pulled out a small wad of notes. 'Here's two hundred. Please take it.'

I shook my head again. 'I can manage.'

The sirens came closer and closer. I rushed to the window and peered out.

I exhaled as a couple of ambulances raced past in the street outside. The sirens started to fade.

Eric walked me down the stairs. 'Be very careful, Cal. I've heard there's even going to be a special airport watch.' He frowned. 'There's a whisper around that you might be trying to leave the country.'

I'd been about to step into the street, but that information froze me mid-step. Why would the police be watching the airports? How did they know I was even thinking of leaving the country? Who had talked?

in Main Street in Carrick, and your dad invited me to dinner at the Clonmel Way Guest House, where he was staying. It's just a little way out of the central part of the village, down along the river. He was beaming about a purchase he'd just made, something he'd paid a lot of money for—found in an antique shop. I figured it was something for your mum.'

The Ormond Jewel, I thought to myself, nodding excitedly. He *did* buy it in Ireland.

'That was probably the last clear memory I have from Ireland,' he said.

There was a silence cut by the sounds of distant sirens. All my muscles tensed. It was time to leave.

'What are you going to do, Cal?'

That was the question I'd been asking myself in some way or another for nearly a year now. I came away from the window and stood in front of his desk. 'I'm going to do what I set out to do. Discover why my dad died. Do whatever it takes to track down the truth about the Ormond Singularity. Discover what it means, clear my name and get my family back together.'

I could see the pity in Eric Blair's eyes. I wondered for a moment whether Dad had confided in him about what happened to my twin. My life so far had been bookended with crime—first the through every cell of my body. 'Someone tried to kill me and my uncle, way back in January,' I said slowly. 'Our fishing boat was sabotaged. Then someone shot Rafe, too, and attacked my sister. The crime that I was blamed for. People have been trying to kill *me* all year. Then there was the sniper at the chapel . . . My family's cursed.'

An awkward half-smile appeared on Eric's lips.

'Hey,' I said, suddenly thinking of something. 'Did you go to college with Dad?'

'That's right, I did. I didn't know him very well. Just knew his name was Tom and that he had a twin brother who was always by his side. I couldn't tell them apart. I didn't meet Tom again until we started working together, many years later.'

Rafe was 'always by his side'? I couldn't imagine it.

'Can you tell me what you remember,' I said, 'about the last time you saw Dad? It doesn't have to be anything important . . . I just like to hear about him.'

I felt grief stir. It hadn't been too active lately, I'd been distracted by so many other things. I pushed it back down.

'For the conference I was staying at the hotel

'Are you suggesting something deliberate?'

'Maybe I've spoken out of place,' Eric said. 'Without proof, I probably should remain silent. Forget it, Cal. I really don't know. All I know is that I was very distressed when I realised Tom had died. He was a great photographer and an even better journalist. He was meticulous about what he wrote. He stood for everything that is good and true. There are not many like him any more.'

It was good to hear that. 'I know,' I said. 'And despite everything you might hear about me, I haven't done anything bad either—I mean, nothing that's harmed another person—not deliberately, anyway. I've just done what I had to. To survive.'

'I believe you, Cal. The frightening thing is,' Eric continued, 'even though I've forgotten everything else, I sense that his illness and mine were somehow connected to the Ormond Singularity.'

'So is that what you meant had killed my dad? That the Ormond Singularity was killing you, too?'

'Possibly. Obviously, with the Ormond name, it's something tied to your family, but maybe I got in the way. Maybe I knew too much. Not that I can remember anything now.'

I thought for a moment and a shiver went

'As sick as I was, I couldn't shake the sense of impending doom—not mine, but *yours*. The Ormond Singularity rings a distant bell.' He shook his head regretfully. 'Unfortunately, I don't know why—I don't know what it is or what it means. This viral infection destroyed a lot of the connectors in my brain. I became even more ill in the new year. I could no longer speak. My thoughts were scrambled . . .'

'That's what happened to my dad,' I said. 'Except he didn't recover. He must have been suffering from a worse case of the virus than you. But,' I reminded him, 'on New Year's Eve, you told me Dad had been murdered, and that I'd be next.' I closed my eyes and tried to remember his words exactly. *'They killed your father. They're killing me!'* I said. 'That's what you said to me. You thought they were killing you, too. Who were you talking about? Who were *they*?'

'All the doctors said it was some unknown viral infection. Something mysterious your dad and I had picked up overseas. I don't understand.'

Eric Blair paused in his pacing, raised his head and gave me a piercing look. 'What if it wasn't an infection, Cal?'

He'd practically taken the words out of my mouth, but it was shocking to hear *him* say it.

'I do recall, though, that Tom told me you were in great danger—you were all in great danger— and then he got sick. Not long after that, I fell ill too. I do, however, feel quite strongly that he wanted me to get the message to you. Perhaps that's why I—'

'Chased me down, New Year's Eve.'

Eric leaned against the desk, his face serious and concerned.

'Yes, but I still don't remember it. I don't know why I said the things I said.' He took a deep breath and continued. 'I feel like Tom had uncovered something in Ireland. Not to do with the conference, necessarily, but more to do with your family. I think he knew it had the capacity to attract the forces of evil. I don't know why, but I feel like the Queen had something to do with it.'

'Yes,' I said, starting to get excited. 'Queen Elizabeth the First!'

'Something to do with her and Ireland,' he added. 'But that's it.'

I sat on the chair under the window, frustrated. I glanced at the yellow daisies, wilting in their vase.

Eric heaved himself back off the desk and walked around, restlessly pacing, hands behind his back, head bowed.

24 NOVEMBER

38 days to go . . .

7:51 am

I was on my way back to Eric Blair's office. He'd called me late last night, asking me to come down to meet him this morning. I could hardly sleep after speaking to him, waiting for the time to come, and hoping for his memory to have returned.

Eric Blair's office

8:32 am

'Cal,' he said, when I walked into his office and eased my backpack off, 'I know you're desperate to clear your name, and get some answers, but I'm afraid I'm going to be a disappointment to you. Ever since our meeting I've been racking my brain, trying to dig deep and piece my memory back together, but it's like driving through impossibly thick fog. I have to keep pulling over.'

My shoulders instantly slumped.

'After all this time, trying to make sense of the Singularity,' I said, 'I am not about to let someone like Sheldrake Rathbone beat me to it.'

'She wasn't sure exactly. Said he left in a bit of a rush. A couple of weeks, maybe. But she did say that after that, he's flying to Dublin. *Ireland*.'

'Damn it,' I swore. 'The Gordian knot.' I jumped to my feet. 'He's going to cut the rope and go straight to wherever the Ormond Singularity is! That's why he must have thrown out the list of remaining nicknames.'

Both of my friends looked at me, confused.

'He must have given up on trying to find the Jewel and the Riddle, and decided to just dive right in and go looking for the Ormond Singularity. Right to the heart of the matter— Ireland!'

'Don't freak out just yet,' said Winter. 'He doesn't know everything we know. He's behind. He's not going to know where to start.'

'He'll talk to other people in Ireland. Someone like Rathbone will have plenty of legal contacts who could be equipped to give him much more information than we have! Remember he's been gathering information on my family for years! He's seen the Piers Ormond letters and he knows the contents of the will. He knows time is ticking down.'

I ripped my hat off and ran my hands through my hair in pure frustration.

'Not after Sligo's banquet. He could recognise me.'

'No, we don't want that happening,' I said.

'I can call Dorothy,' said Winter. 'See if I can squeeze any handy info out of her. Who knows what she could tell me.'

She stood up and brushed sand off her legs.

'No time like the present,' she exclaimed, pulling out her phone. 'I think Dorothy's there until twelve on Saturdays.'

Winter shook some more sand from her hands, then made the call. She wandered away to a quieter spot.

I watched her. The girl had everything brains, beauty and courage.

11:56 am

Boges and I waited expectantly as she finally returned. The minute I saw her face, I knew something was wrong.

'Wasn't Dorothy there?'

Winter plonked herself back down on the towel beside us. 'Man, that woman can talk,' she said. 'She was there—that wasn't the problem. Rathbone's gone.' Her forehead gathered in a worried frown. 'She says the office is all quiet again because he's flown to London.'

'For how long?' I asked.

20 NOVEMBER

42 days to go . . .

11:15 am

The three of us sat on the beach. Winter was making lines in the sand with her toe. We were wearing wide-brimmed hats to protect us from the sun, but also to stop any unwanted attention coming our way.

Boges, who was never a huge fan of the beach, was lying back, watching people come and go around us. Down near the water, little kids played, building sandcastles, running from the waves and picking up shells, while seagulls swooped over the brilliant blue sea.

'We have to put pressure on Rathbone,' said Boges, 'and force him to tell us who those other nicknames belong to. You got on really well with his assistant, Dorothy, didn't you, Winter? Cal said you two were talking up a storm while he was hiding under Rathbone's desk.'

'I can't risk Rathbone seeing me,' she replied. She reached into her bag for some sunscreen.

He nodded. 'Of course. I'm sorry I scared you. I don't know what else to say right now.'

'That's OK. Let's talk again soon.'

Fit For Life

5:01 pm

'We just have to trust the forger,' said Sharkey, quickly counting the money. 'As much as I don't really want to deal with him—it means I'm tiptoeing on the wrong side of the law, and I've avoided that for all of my career—he has a good reputation. I don't think he'll give us any trouble.'

He's a *criminal*, I thought. I was dealing with a forger—a specialist in deceit—but I had no choice. I had to part with the money and hope he'd come through.

Sharkey must have suspected the doubt that was going through my mind. 'It's not in his interest to double-cross a customer,' he said. 'People would stop dealing with him if he did that. Even a forger needs a good business reputation. I'll call you again as soon as the job is done.'

'Yes, keep trying to remember,' I urged.

'In Ireland, Tom was very close . . . close to discovering what it was.'

At the mention of Ireland, hope was returning.

'Mr Blair, why do you think everything is so blurry? What was wrong with you?'

'I get flashes,' he said, 'like the jagged reflections you might get in a shattered mirror, but mostly it's a blur. I was with your dad in Ireland when I fell ill. We both did. It was near the end of our trip, but for some reason I don't remember any of the trip clearly. I had some awful viral infection in my brain and spent a long time in hospital.'

'You told me my dad was *killed*.'

'Killed?' Eric Blair rested his head in his hands. He looked really pale. 'This has all come as a huge shock to me,' he said. 'I was anxious about meeting you, but I had no idea this was coming. I'm going to need some time to digest it all.'

My mobile rang. It was Nelson Sharkey. 'Excuse me,' I said to Eric, before taking the call.

'Everything is ready to go,' said Sharkey. 'All we need now is the money. Can you meet me at the gym in an hour?'

'I'm on my way,' I said.

Blair was still shell-shocked, behind his desk. 'I have to go, Mr Blair, but can you please call me as soon as anything comes back to you?'

365 days. It's been haunting me ever since. My life took a dive-bomb almost instantly.'

'Please, come back to the office. Let's sit down and get to the bottom of this.'

3:25 pm

'Sit down, Cal. Here,' he said, pulling out a chair. He was frowning, straining to remember a scene that he had starred in—one I remembered with all its vivid terror.

'You really don't remember staggering along the street near my house, yelling out my name? Warning me about the Ormond Singularity?'

'*The Ormond Singularity*,' he muttered, ominously.

'Last year, on New Year's Eve? You don't remember the paramedics who came after you and carted you off in an ambulance?'

'I *was* sick then . . .' he said, trying so hard to make sense of this. The expression on his face slowly transformed from confusion into a steadier gaze, as if he'd managed to pin something down in his memory. 'The Ormond Singularity, the Ormond Singularity,' he chanted. 'I think I remember something about that phrase now. There *was* something called the Ormond Singularity . . . something to do with Tom.'

Eric was nodding now.

I've never met you before in my life! 365 days?' he murmured to himself. '*365 days?*' he repeated.

I wrenched the door open and took off.

'Cal! Come back!' Eric yelled down the corridor. 'What do you mean? *365 days?* Please, come back! Help me understand! Don't run away like this!'

I was down the stairs and back out on the street when I realised Eric was coming after me. I turned back and his image instantly merged into that of the staggering sick man who had already chased me once.

'I want to help you! You have nothing to fear from me,' he shouted. 'Tom was my friend!'

All of a sudden my body just stopped running. My mind was sending me danger signals, but my heart told me to turn around and hear him out.

Blair bent over—puffed out, helpless and completely harmless. As he stood upright again, I thought I could see tears in his eyes.

'365 days,' he repeated, yet again. 'I don't know why, but for some reason that is strangely familiar to me. But why?' he said in a barely audible voice, as though he was thinking aloud.

'That's because *you* were the one who said it to me. You told me my dad had been murdered and that I would be too if I didn't hide out for

I dropped his hand.

'You OK?' he asked, his eyes alarmed at my retreat.

I recognised the confusion and worry in his eyes and backed away faster, reaching behind me for the door.

'What is it?' he asked.

He stepped towards me.

'Get away from me,' I growled.

'Cal, what's the problem? You're safe in here. Why the sudden change of heart?'

'I said, get away from me.'

I was dizzy. Flashbacks from that hot December afternoon, New Year's Eve, fired into my mind.

'You!' I shouted, unable to control my voice. 'It was *you*! *You* were the crazy guy that chased me down my street last year! *You* were the one who told me I had 365 days to survive, that they killed my father, that they'd kill me too!'

'What? Cal—'

'I can't believe it! After all this time! This 365-day countdown *began* with you!'

Although he looked different, I could still see the wildness in his eyes.

Eric's face was a mixture of concern and bewilderment.

'Cal,' he said, 'what are you talking about?

Eric Blair's office

Even with my dark brown contacts, I avoided looking anyone in the eye as I made my way back down to the docks, to Eric Blair's personal office.

I didn't feel as anxious about this meeting as I did last time, but I was still carefully scoping the scene, making sure I wasn't about to be sprung by the cops, or some other thug.

Eric's office was located in a modern building with the foyer opening directly onto the footpath. I strolled on in and up the stairs to the second floor. I took a deep breath before knocking on the door marked number seven.

'Come in,' he called.

I took another deep breath and walked in.

I'd stepped into a small office with one window overlooking the water. A vase of bright yellow daisies sat on his relatively empty desk. Eric stood up from behind the desk as I tentatively approached him, offering him my hand.

'Good to finally meet you,' I said.

'And you too, son,' he said, shaking my hand. His smile was warm and friendly, but I suddenly felt uneasy.

I stopped in my tracks.

I jumped on the library's online newspaper files, and looked up Kenthurst and the date of the abduction.

TWIN TRAGEDY

One month on from the shocking abduction of twin boys from Kenthurst on 11 November, Rafe Ormond has come forward to make a plea to the public for privacy.

'It's been an extremely difficult time for the family,' he said in a press conference, earlier today. 'A struggle that has, so far, been without end. All I can ask is for people to please respect Winifred and Tom's need for privacy. To have one baby returned to you, without knowing what happened to the other . . . it's a parent's worst nightmare. Tom and I are twins, obviously,' he continued, 'and the thought of being separated from him, even as an adult, is . . . too painful to imagine. My brother and I are so close—inseparable—and we always have been. The bond between twins is . . . indescribable. We're like each other's shadow. I am simply not me without him. I just pray that baby Samuel is returned to us, safely, and that Callum has the chance to grow up with his twin beside him.'

At this point, Rafe Ormond—who was visibly upset—abruptly stood up and walked away from the reporters, cutting the interview short.

I pushed my chair away from the monitor. This wasn't the Rafe I knew. For as long as I could remember he and dad were almost *strangers*. They weren't each other's shadows. Was he just playing the media? Or had the tragedy changed him?

'No idea. But he was right about me feeling unsure of him.'

'One person I think you should speak to is Rathbone,' he said. 'We have to make him talk, and tell us who the nicknames belong to.'

'He won't do it—not without a lot of pressure.'

'Pressure is what we have. We still have the photos of him with his dirty money,' he reminded me. 'It worked once, it can work again. You don't have a problem with breaking a promise to a criminal, do you?'

'I guess not,' I said. 'But what will make him trust us this time? What will make him give anything to us when we could just go back on our word again, and bribe him with the photos for something else?'

'Dude, he can't take the risk of those photos getting out. He's up to no good, and I'm pretty sure he won't want to jeopardise that extra income he's been generating on the sly.'

10:32 am

I snuck out to go to the local library, careful to avoid the Lovetts on my way. It seemed Luke's parents were having a bit of a clean-up in the yard. I made sure my cash-loaded backpack was strapped on tight, and hoped they'd steer clear of the treehouse.

get me. 'I hope you never regret this, Boges,' I said.

'What do you mean?'

'If I don't clear my name, and the cops find out about your association with me, that could totally finish off any dreams you have of an internship with NASA. It could blow your education.'

Boges looked serious. 'Then we've got our work cut out for us, haven't we? Now,' he said looking around, lifting his camera out of his bag, 'where's the best place to set up the passport photo shoot?'

I grabbed the contact lens case Winter had given me, and jumped out of the tree to go wash my hands at the tap. After a lot of trouble, I finally got the slippery suckers into my eyes. Blinking, I looked up at Boges.

Boges blinked back. 'They make you look really weird. So different. Come up here and I'll take the pic in front of the curtains.'

After he'd taken a few, I peered over his shoulder at my image on the screen of his camera. The guy who stared back at me wasn't me.

'These will do. I'll fix them up a bit on my computer, then I'd better give them to Sharkey. So tell me,' he said, sitting back down again, 'what do you think Rafe wants to talk to you about?'

knowing you, and I didn't know anything about this!' Boges's eyebrows were up at his hairline, and his round face was shocked and concerned.

'Neither did I! It's like I've tripped over and fallen into a parallel universe. The life I've known is not my real life. Everything's been kept a secret from me, to protect me from the memory.'

'So it happened in Kenthurst—you must have lived there before Richmond. Your parents must have moved to escape the attention from the tragedy. That must be why no-one who lives near you has ever mentioned this massive crime happening to you guys. If only everyone knew who you were! But who ordered the kidnapping?' Boges asked. 'Who paid Toecutter to wipe out you and your brother?'

'He didn't say. Maybe I'll never find out.' I paused. 'He never got paid for it, anyway. He never finished the job.'

'Griff Kirby must be working for him now. He's moved up in the world pretty fast. Gone from petty crime to the big time. He could be the next Toecutter. Wow,' said Boges, shaking his head. 'This is nuts! I can't believe you really have a twin!'

'Believe it. I'm going to have to tell Ryan about it some day soon. He deserves to know the truth, too.' I thought about the new strike force out to

18 NOVEMBER

44 days to go . . .

7:20 am

Boges hissed my name and I threw him the rope.

Soon his figure appeared at the window and he squeezed his way through, dropping down opposite me.

'Dude, what is it? What's happened?'

I told him about my run-in with Ezekiel and how I'd been hauled into Toecutter's bedroom for his confession. I also told him how my mum had reacted, and about Rafe's mysterious message, cut short on the phone.

I handed Boges the yellowing newspaper clipping.

Boges read it in a few moments, then looked up in disbelief.

'You and your brother were kidnapped by Toecutter? Ryan Spencer is Samuel, your twin brother? I can't get my head around this!' Boges sat there, staring at me. 'All these years of are making jokes. Imagine what the international agents will think. The newspaper cartoonists are having a field day. Now they're going to have teams of volunteers as well as cops reviewing all the public closed-circuit cameras on a daily basis. They're gunning for you. More than ever.'

'Sounds like I need your help, more than ever. Please say you'll meet me. I'll make it quick, I promise. I won't bring any trouble to you. Can we try again?'

It took some convincing, but Eric Blair finally agreed to another meeting. He told me it was my last shot—that he was too concerned about being caught with me. I wasn't going to let that be a problem.

Eric Blair!

I jumped up so hard I banged my head on the roof of the treehouse. I'd stood him up!

I pulled my mobile out and dialled his number. It went straight to voicemail.

'Eric, er, it's me. I'm so sorry I didn't show up for our meeting,' I said. 'I can't believe I missed it. I was on my way when—'

'Hello? Cal?' said Eric, suddenly picking up the phone.

'Eric! Please tell me you'll meet me another time? I won't mess up again, I swear.'

'I know it can't be easy for a fugitive to keep his appointments, but I have to admit, I'm apprehensive about giving it another go. The police called a news briefing this morning with all the leading journos of the city. If you thought the arrest of Oriana de la Force was going to take the heat off you, you're going to have to think again. It seems to have only fuelled the fire.'

I swore.

'Senior Sergeant McGrath told us again how seriously the force is committed to your capture,' Eric continued, 'especially with a huge international security convention being held in the Harbour next month. McGrath's created a new strike force—*Predator*. He's furious about being thwarted by a sixteen-year-old kid. Colleagues

'Mum,' I said. 'I've found him. He's alive.'

The shocked silence at the other end of the line deepened into a huge void.

'Mum?' I asked.

'Samuel? He's alive? Please don't lie to me, Cal,' she pleaded, the distress obvious in her voice.

'I'm not, I promise. I've met him. He looks just like me. He's fine. He's had a good life—I want you to know that.'

I could hear her crying on the phone and I was feeling overcome with all sorts of strange and powerful emotions. 'I can't talk any more,' I said, swallowing hard. 'I just wanted you to know that Samuel's OK. And in case you still care,' I added, before hanging up, 'I am, too.'

9:00 pm

Not so long ago, I'd have gone to my mum if something was bothering me. Not even for advice, necessarily, but because she had that knack of making me feel better. I had almost forgotten what that felt like.

Something in the back of my mind was telling me that I was forgetting an important detail. I was processing so much information that I couldn't pinpoint it.

There was somewhere I was supposed to be . . . someone I was supposed to see . . .

she's still finding it hard to cope with her family in tatters.'

'This could help.'

Rafe paused. 'Do you mean you're going to hand yourself in?' he asked, hopefully.

'I can't do that.'

I heard my uncle sigh. 'If it's important,' he said, 'why don't you give me your message and I'll pass it on to her. I think it'd be better if she heard it from me, speaking on your behalf.'

'Please, just let me talk to her.'

'Cal, I need to speak to you myself—man to man.' His voice was a whisper. 'I want you to know that *I* know—'

He was cut short. I could hear my mum calling.

'Is that Cal? Let me speak to him! It's my son!'

Within seconds she was running to the phone, but not before Rafe spoke urgently. 'I know you don't quite trust me, but you should. If we could—'

But it was too late. Mum had grabbed the phone from him.

'Cal? Where are you?' she blurted.

'It doesn't matter where I am. Mum, I need to tell you something. I know everything. I know about the abduction when I was a baby. That I had a twin who was never found.'

I heard my mum's sharp intake of breath on the other end of the line.

Then I got to thinking about whether Mum would *want* to be reunited with her lost son. It would mean Ryan finding out about his shocking past, having to face the fact that the woman who had raised him was not his biological mother.

'Hi Mum,' I imagined myself saying to her. 'I have something amazing to tell you. I found Samuel.'

I rehearsed it over and over, trying out different ways of breaking this massive news to her.

Finally, still undecided as to how I was going to put it, I retrieved my phone and dialled Rafe's place.

'Rafe speaking.'

'Uncle Rafe, it's me.'

'Cal?' he replied, his voice quavering.

'Please hear me out. First of all, I just want to say that I didn't fire the gun at the chapel. I'd heard a sniper was going to try to take you out, so I went there to stop him. To save you.'

'Wh-where are you?' he stuttered. 'Are you OK?'

'I'm fine. Listen, I really need to speak to Mum. I have something important to tell her. Something I think she'll want to hear.'

'I hope it's not something that will upset her. Every time she talks to you, she ends up in a mess. She's fragile, Cal. She has Gabbi back, but their dark secrets, and why they treated me as though I was *damaged*. They thought I was scarred from the trauma, even though I was way too young at the time to remember it clearly. At last I understood why I always felt like something was missing.

I had a brother. Ryan Spencer's mum was a friend of Durham's sister. My double was my twin.

The name my parents had given him was *Samuel*.

7:56 pm

Head down, my mind still whirling from Toecutter's confession, I found my way back to the treehouse. I snuck up to the Lovetts' shed to plug my phone in for a charge, then hauled myself up the tree and collapsed on the floor.

My head was thumping. A song suddenly drifted into my thoughts.

'Two little lambs in the cold night frost, one was saved and the other one lost.'

Great-aunt Millicent's song must have been her attempt to tell me about my brother.

The soft wind stirred the leaves of the huge tree outside the windows. I sat up on the bench and hugged my knees. I had to call Mum. I had to tell her about Ryan—about *Samuel*. She needed to know that her other son was alive and well.

TWIN BABY ABDUCTION NIGHTMARE

Police said today that they have no new leads in the now year-old kidnap case involving twin boys, Callum and Samuel Ormond.

Callum Ormond, the older twin, was discovered some time after the kidnapping. He was found on the floor of an abandoned building near the old Kenthurst Town Hall. It is not known what happened to the child before he was located. The younger twin, Samuel Ormond, remains missing. To date, no ransom note has been produced. Samuel's fate is unknown, but police hold grave fears for his safety. The twins' parents, Winifred and Thomas Ormond, say they cannot under-

THE TWINS BEFORE THEY WERE TRAGICALLY SEPARATED

stand why this has happened to them. They pray every day for the safe return of their missing son, so that their family can be whole again.

I leaned my head back against the wall of one of the bins. The newspaper clipping trembled in my shaky hands. As sick as all of this was making me, understanding brought an overwhelming sense of relief. At last I had the explanation as to why that threadbare white toy dog, the cold building and the crying baby had brought such fear and desolation to my nightmares. At last I understood why Mum and Rafe wanted to keep

'What are you raving about, boy? I don't know what you're talking about.'

From somewhere in the house, I heard a door slam. Immediately, the sick old man became agitated. 'Ezekiel! Ezekiel? Get in here now!'

The Polynesian suddenly appeared at the door.

'That's Wayne coming home!' said Durham. 'Get this kid out of here! Use the back door. Oh, I almost forgot! Wait, son, take this with you.'

With that, Murray Durham, his haggard face pale with fear, opened a bedside drawer, took out an envelope and pushed it into my hand. 'Now, disappear, the pair of you!'

Ezekiel grabbed me and hurried me to the door, looking out each way, like he was checking for traffic.

'Follow me,' urged Ezekiel, before racing me down the hallway towards the door at the end. He kicked it open. 'On your way!' he said, pushing me out. 'Disappear! Fast!'

I didn't have to be told twice. With the envelope tucked tightly under my arm, I took off, running.

5:20 pm

After I'd put a bit of distance between me and Murray Durham, I found a place to hide—in a carpark behind some charity bins—and ripped the envelope open.

wanted you to realise who you were. I wanted you to know about the other boy—your twin. But then I ended up sending Ezekiel and Chook to find you and bring you in so I could tell you myself.'

I was speechless.

'I've felt bad all my life about taking those kids—bad about that mum losing one of her boys, bad about separating twins. And now that I'm an old man, I finally understand the damage I did to that family, stealing their children like that, tearing them apart. So anyway,' he said, taking a big breath, 'I needed you to know the truth . . . while I was still able to tell it to you. I feel better now,' he whispered, barely audible. 'I feel lighter already.'

'Who was the person who hired you to do the contract job?' I asked.

Durham was silent.

'Who was it?' I asked again, thinking of the list of names from Rathbone's office. My shock was suddenly being overtaken by anger. This guy had ripped me off from having a life of grow-ing up with my brother. He'd taken us from our parents, and my twin—Ryan—had never been returned. 'Who ordered the kidnapping? Was it someone called Deep Water, or Double Trouble, or The Little Prince? Tell me!'

have children, and together we organised dodgy adoption papers.'

'What happened to the other baby?' I asked. 'The one your partner left behind?'

'He was eventually found by the cops. He was cold and hungry, but he was fine.' Durham stopped speaking and stared at me. 'He was reunited with his family late that night.' His bloodshot eyes examined mine. 'You've probably guessed by now who the child was.'

A sick feeling welled up in my stomach as so many of the unexplained things from my life started falling horribly into place.

I was the child who was returned.

Durham's eyes continued to bore through me.

'Sandy's friend never knew any different. She took the other baby, and the white toy dog he was clutching when we took him, and thought the adoption was legal and above board. She never knew that Sandy was the sister of Toecutter Durham.'

The white toy dog of my nightmares—the dog I'd discovered in Ryan Spencer's room—started making more sense.

'The abduction happened on the eleventh of November. The date I left on your blog.'

'You did that? You hacked my blog?'

'I wanted you to investigate the date. I

The cop car returned so I slammed my foot on the accelerator and sped off. I drove all the way back to my place, and just as I stepped inside, my sister Sandra turned up—she was living with me at the time. There I was with a damn baby screaming his head off. I couldn't think quick enough to make up a story about the predicament she'd caught me in. She was horrified at what I'd done. She'd raised me—was like a mum to me—and she was furious. She'd just heard about the kidnapping on the radio and couldn't believe someone would do such a thing . . . let alone me. Her little brother. Turns out my partner had abandoned the other baby in the old house, and made a run for it alone.'

The old man's lips quivered at the memory.

'I didn't know what to do with the baby. He wouldn't stop crying. I had to keep him quiet and out of sight so the neighbours wouldn't suspect anything. I begged Sandy to help me. Regretfully, she took the little guy from me and calmed him down. She was great with him. She fed him, and put him to sleep. Before we knew it, days had passed, then weeks, then months. Sandy had fallen in love with him. I told her we couldn't keep him any longer, that she had to get him out of the house. But she had nowhere else to take him. Finally she found a friend who couldn't

He glared at me, as if daring me to contradict him.

'I should never have agreed to it,' he continued. 'My heart was never in it and maybe that's why the whole thing was a disaster. The job never felt right, but I'd grown accustomed to luxury and got greedy. Plus I had an old debt that I wanted cleared, and I saw this as my opportunity to finally knock it out. It's sad what people will do for money. How much of themselves they're willing to sacrifice to get the things they want. I didn't see a cent in the end. It was all for nothing. I was working with a partner—he's dead now—and we broke into the Kenthurst house—'

'Kenthurst?' I blurted out. I thought I understood what he was talking about, but my family was from Richmond.

'Kenthurst,' he repeated. 'We picked up the two sleeping babies without any trouble, then drove off to an old building that I knew was waiting for demolition. We'd just made it inside and put the babies down when I spotted a police patrol car on the street. The babies were crying and I panicked. I ordered my partner to grab one of them, while I grabbed the other, and we split. I ran out to the car, thinking my partner was following me, but he wasn't. I waited behind the wheel for him, but I didn't see him come out of the building.

'Don't be scared of me. This old dog is dying, can't you see? No teeth. No bite.' He knocked his fingers against the glass of water containing his false teeth. 'Anyway, I'm done for, son. I don't have any action left in me, good or bad, except to make a long-overdue confession. So come on. Spit it out.'

'My guess is you were involved in the abduction of twin boys,' I said. 'Sixteen years ago.'

I waited, holding my breath. There was a long silence.

Durham cleared his throat and shifted on his satin pillows.

'You're right on the money,' he admitted. 'I *was* part of that notorious kidnapping.'

My heart was racing. I tried to focus and listen carefully to his every word.

'I was a well-known hitman by that stage of my life, and I was approached by someone with an unusual assignment. My job was to kidnap twin babies from a suburban house, and dispose of them. I was offered a fair amount of money in return, but that's when I discovered something about myself—the infamous, heartless Murray Durham didn't have it in him to be a baby killer. Yeah, I could cut the toes off dirty crooks and homicidal jailbirds, but I couldn't harm a baby. I suppose that's a good thing.'

He started to laugh, making a choking, rusty sound like it was something he hadn't done in a while.

'He'd probably kill you too. So we'd better make this quick, while he's out of the place.'

'Let's do that,' I agreed.

Again came the rusty, choking sound of his laugh. He reached for his water once more. I helped it to his lips.

Durham had said this terrible event occurred sixteen years ago. Things started coming together in my mind. I pictured the newspaper clipping about the abduction of twin babies that Great-uncle Bartholomew had snatched out of my hands. I pictured Ryan and his mum. I pictured *my* mum and the sadness in her eyes.

'I think I know what you're talking about, Mr Durham,' I said slowly.

'Is that right?' he asked, dubiously.

'Are you talking about a kidnapping?'

His eyebrows rose, slowly. 'Smart kid, eh? I'm not surprised you have some idea about it; you've been able to avoid the cops and the crims for nearly a year. So tell me, what do you think *you* have to do with it?'

I wasn't too sure what to say. Murray Durham might be the sort of guy who could lash out in rage if someone made a mistake about him.

Not really, I thought in my head. But it didn't matter—Durham wasn't waiting for an answer.

'I used to cut off people's toes with bolt cutters. If they got in my way, owed me money, messed with someone in my crew.' Durham shook his head, clearly disturbed by his violent past. 'They were all crims, in one way or another, and some of them were just as vicious as me. But there's this one thing I did that I can't get out of my mind. This world is an unforgiving place. And I can't forgive myself for it.'

His head fell back on the pillows as if he were exhausted from the effort of talking.

'Sixteen years ago, now,' he said. 'And it's been something I've found almost impossible to live with. Now that I'm coming to the end of my life, I realise it's not something I can *die* with, either.'

A noise at the door startled Durham. 'What was that?' he asked.

'Nothing to worry about,' I said, wondering why he was so edgy.

'As long as it's not my son. He thinks I'm crazy wanting to tell you about this. I can't let him catch me with you.'

About this? What was he talking about? Had he lost his mind?

'He'd kill me,' he said. 'It wouldn't take much!'

I had a good brain, the teachers used to tell me, but I didn't listen to them. What would they know, I thought to myself. I'd never really done anything bad before that, but after the car-jacking I thought I was tough and cool and the king of the streets in my neighbourhood. See, I didn't know then what it meant to get a bad name, or a police record. I didn't realise that one event could change the path of my life forever.'

Durham looked at his glass of water. I leaned over and passed it to him.

'Thanks,' he said, awkwardly passing it back to me. 'Some years later, I tried to turn my life around. I began studying and earned some quali-fications at a technical college. But no-one wanted to employ me. My criminal convictions got in the way. Do you understand what I'm trying to tell you? I couldn't even travel. No country would let me enter because of my record.' His piercing eyes bored into me from their hollow sockets. 'I felt I had no choice but to return to crime, where I grew into a monster.'

'My reputation is all bad too,' I said, 'and I didn't even commit the crimes I've been accused of.'

'I'm afraid I can't say that for my crimes,' admitted the old man. 'You wanna know how I got my nickname?'

room and raced to the choking man's side. The nurse picked up an inhaler from the floor and helped Durham insert it in his mouth. He took some desperate breaths, sucked in the vapour from the inhaler, and soon his wild eyes relaxed, and the coughing eased.

'You mustn't tire yourself, Mr Durham,' the nurse scolded, looking across at me disapprovingly, as he plumped up the pillows behind the old man's head.

'I'm all right now,' Durham replied, sipping from a glass of water. 'I'll call you if I need you again. Leave me now.'

With a frown, the nurse left the room.

I sat down on a chair that rested beside the bed. When Durham started speaking again, his voice was even weaker. I leaned in closer to him.

'When you're young, you don't understand,' he said. 'You can't see the future, so you don't consider how one wrong choice can lead to a life like mine—the life of a career criminal.'

I thought of Repro and how he was now forced to live underground, on the run from the very man who lay dying in front of me. He'd made a bad decision to use his skills in the service of criminals.

'When I did my first car-jacking, I was sixteen.

I didn't want to admit that I was. 'Why did you bring me here?' I asked, avoiding the question.

'You're a brave lad, I can tell that. But you don't have anything to fear from me. Understood?'

I didn't say anything, but he continued anyway.

'I've committed many crimes in my life. So many bad, bad things. And I know I'll face the consequences when I go to meet my maker. But before that time comes, there's something I need to get off my chest.'

He paused again, and my mind was searching for a reason why I was standing by his bed, listening to him reflect on his life.

'Most of the bad things I did because I had to,' he said. 'This is a tough city and if you want to stay on top, you have to be tougher than everybody else. You can't let things get to you. I don't regret the things I did to keep my affairs in order, exactly. But there has always been one thing I've never quite been able to . . . to *live* with.'

A terrible coughing fit suddenly convulsed through Durham's body, and his claw-like hands groped around for something. I looked to the door, about to call for help, when a young male nurse, stethoscope bumping on his chest, ran into the

I could tell from the skin hanging loose on his face that he'd lost a lot of weight, and even in the shadows I could see bruising around his eyes. His skin was grey—like the haggard appearances of my dad and of Great-uncle Bartholomew, just before they died. Magnified in a glass of water by the bed were his false teeth.

'Are you Callum Ormond, son?' he asked. His voice, although gruff, was weak and almost kind.

'I am,' I said. There was no point in denying it.

For a long moment, he stared at me, silently. I shifted uncomfortably until finally he spoke again.

'I'm dying, son.'

I didn't know what to say. I just hoped that his last wish wasn't to rid the world of Callum Ormond.

'What do you have to say about that?' he urged.

'I'm sorry to hear it,' I said, awkwardly.

'You needn't be sorry. It's something we all have to go through. Death is cruel—so very cruel—but life cannot exist without it. I haven't lived a good life, son. I've done a lot of bad things. Things that were against the law—unspeakable things. People have feared me all my life. Are you afraid of me?'

Finally we paused outside a closed door. The Polynesian knocked on it, surprisingly softly. 'The boss is not a well man,' he whispered to me. 'I'm just warning you.'

Warning *me*?

From inside I heard a faint voice.

'Who is it?'

'Ezekiel, boss. Got the kid with me.'

With that, Ezekiel opened the door and pushed me inside.

I stumbled into the room. I had to blink because I couldn't see properly. The room was dark—darker even than Dr Leporello's creepy fungi study. Once my eyes adjusted, I could just make out the figure of a man lying in a king-size dark timber bed, draped in red satin. He heaved himself up, leaning crookedly on his pillows.

'Come over here, kid. Where I can see you.'

Ezekiel, the big Polynesian, nodded at me, telling me to do as Durham said.

I stepped up to the end of the bed and started taking in the features of the sick person in front of me. At one point, Murray Durham had been a big man, but I remembered that he'd looked pretty frail and sick at Sligo's banquet. Now he looked ten times worse. My body was shaking, but I stood tall, hoping that the courage of Piers Ormond would get me through whatever might happen next.

The car pulled up in a garage, and the door closed behind us. I was pulled out and escorted along an endless terrace. The lawns of this place were as big as the Botanical Gardens, planted with rows and rows of trees, and dotted with hedges carved into incredible shapes—camels, rearing horses, a T-rex, the Statue of Liberty and a racing car. 'Topiary' was the name of this manicured way of shaping trees, I recalled, wondering how I could remember something so useless at a time like this.

After a lengthy march along the terrace, we finally came to an elaborate marbled entrance. The house looked like a smaller version of Buckingham Palace.

My captors hauled me through the doors and into what looked like acres of marbled floors, decorated with lavish gold and velvet furniture. On the walls hung enormous old oil paintings and tapestries. In the middle of this acreage, a huge, white fountain splashed water into a circular pool filled with colourful koi fish.

'This way,' said the Polynesian, keeping a firm hold on my arm as we walked down an endless hallway. The driver of the car had disappeared.

'Where are we going?' I asked.

'Like I said, the boss wants a private chat with you. I'm taking you to him.'

and I shivered. I was convinced I was experiencing my last moments alive. I'd never meet with Eric Blair, I'd never see Mum, Rafe and Gabbi again, or Boges and Winter.

These thoughts turned me ferocious. I went totally feral, punching, lashing out, kicking, trying to get into the front seat. If I could just wrench the wheel around, and crash the car, I could make a break for it. But the big Polynesian hauled me back. As I looked at his face, he didn't look that threatening. He actually looked a bit concerned.

'It's OK, kid,' he said. 'Nobody wants to hurt you. The boss just wants to have a little talk with you.'

'I don't believe you,' I said, trying to keep my voice firm. 'What does he want to talk to me about?'

'It's a personal matter,' muttered the Polynesian. 'Private and personal. Just wait until you meet with him, OK?'

The limousine finally slowed, turning into a driveway as tall, automatic gates opened to let us through. Panicked thoughts raced through my mind. Did Durham want to know something about the Ormond Singularity? Maybe he'd torture me to find out . . .

But Rathbone had crossed 'Toecutter' *off* his list.

I stuck my legs out and gripped the roof of the car with my hands. But a sudden kick behind the knees, combined with a hard shove, collapsed me completely and I was bundled into the back of the limo.

'Who are you? What do you want with me?' I yelled, struggling uselessly as the burly Polynesian practically sat on me. The car took off with great speed.

'If you just behave, calm down and be a good boy, we'll tell you,' said the other guy, now behind the wheel.

'Fine, go on.'

'Murray Durham wants a word with you.'

At the sound of that name, I went limp. Murray 'Toecutter' Durham! Murray Durham was the biggest and most powerful criminal in the country. Sligo must have called in a favour, or paid Durham to take me down. Or, worse, what if Durham wanted me dead himself? That's when I recognised the driver—he was one of Toecutter's bodyguards! He was the one who was watching a war movie on the couch on the night Winter and I broke into her old house to retrieve her locket. He'd also been at Sligo's interrupted banquet, alongside his boss.

I was in real trouble. And Griff Kirby had fingered me. Fear iced over every cell in my body

Too late! Two burly men, one a huge Polynesian guy with long, shiny black hair, and the other an equally bulky guy whose face was vaguely familiar, were about to pounce on me.

'That's Ormond! That's him!' yelled Griff, pointing me out.

I glared at him. *The rat!*

I swore out loud, twisting away and trying to run, but I'd missed my chance! My shock at Griff's betrayal robbed me of vital seconds. I should have known better! The two guys quickly overpowered me. One of them had me in a head-lock, while the other lifted my legs and dragged me towards a car—a black limousine that looked like a hearse.

'Let go of me!' I shouted, kicking and struggling as hard as I could. Then I thought of Eric Blair—had he set this up?

But our meeting wasn't for another few hours. It was early, way too early for it to be a set-up. Wasn't it? Either way, Griff Kirby would pay for this.

'It's OK, boy. Stop struggling and you won't get hurt,' said a gruff voice in my ear.

'It's like trying to wrestle a giant electric eel!' said the other guy. 'Relax, kid!'

'If you want me to relax, let me go!' I shouted, trying to brace myself so that they'd have a hard time getting me into the car.

17 NOVEMBER

45 days to go . . .

2:20 pm

I set off towards the address Eric Blair had given me, wearing a new light-grey hoodie pulled around my face. I'd told Eric I'd be coming with no expectations, but that wasn't entirely true. I was totally counting on this guy giving me valuable information about my dad and maybe even the Ormond Singularity.

I was a few hours early—we'd arranged to meet at six—but I wanted to scope the place out thoroughly before approaching the office, making sure I wasn't walking into a trap. At the slightest hint of danger, I wanted to be able to bolt.

Just as I was thinking this, I spotted Griff Kirby across the road, staring hard at me.

A jolt of fear tore through me. What was he up to this time?

Then I saw he wasn't staring at me, but beyond me. The hairs on the back of my neck stood up and I swung round.

I hesitated, trying to picture the location he was talking about, and how safe it would be for me.

'You'd be safe,' he said, like a mind-reader, 'as long as you're only interested in talking.'

His voice was warm and friendly, even though he kept it very low.

'I mean you no harm,' I reassured him. 'It's just that there's a lot of mystery surrounding Dad's death and his final movements in Ireland. I'm desperate to find out anything you can possibly tell me about your trip with him. That's all I'm after, I swear.'

'Cal, your dad was one of my dearest friends. I always admired his work, his integrity and his love for his family. I'm happy to meet you, but to be honest, I don't know that I have much insight to offer you, so please don't get your hopes up.'

'Give me a time and the address,' I said, 'and I'll be there. No expectations.'

5:06 pm

I sat back on the treehouse bench, eating hand-fuls of peanuts. I had plenty of time to think about how to approach Eric Blair before our meeting, but I was already getting anxious. I couldn't imagine a friend of Dad's being a bad guy. But these days, trust was hard to come by.

but I had to take the risk. I grabbed my phone and dialled his office number.

'You're back,' I said, automatically, when he answered. 'It's Callum Ormond here.'

'Hello, Callum,' he replied, slowly.

'I don't know if I can trust you and you're probably thinking the same thing about me, but I really need to talk to you. Sooner rather than later. I'm running out of time.'

He was quiet.

'Do you trust me?' I blurted out.

'I don't believe everything I've read,' he answered calmly.

'Well that's a start.'

'I just saw on the news that Oriana de la Force has been charged again for the kidnapping of your little sister. I don't believe you were involved in that.'

'Good, because I wasn't,' I said. 'I've only ever wanted to protect her. Will you meet up with me? Somewhere secluded? Somewhere safe?'

Eric was silent for a moment.

'Listen, I have a suggestion,' he said. 'I have a personal office space—just one small room, down near the waterside. I used to use it as a base for freelance work, but these days it's more like a storage unit. No-one has access to it but me. I could meet you there?'

alleges he attacked her,' I read, 'and "violated her face". She has vowed to fight the charges once more, insisting sixteen-year-old Callum Ormond was responsible for the kidnapping of his sister, and that she can prove it. De la Force has been released on bail pending further court appearances.'

I quickly headed away from the newsstand as a few people gathered around to see the headline.

Some crazy thoughts started rushing through my mind. If the cops had evidence proving Oriana was responsible for Gabbi's kidnapping, maybe the bigger truth would come out and my name would be cleared. The authorities would realise I'm innocent. Surely my mum would see that too.

Treehouse

4:24 pm

It felt like a lifetime had passed since I'd spoken to Dad's old colleague Eric Blair, and I couldn't believe it had taken a reminder from Winter to make me call him again. He'd been a tough guy to get in touch with. First he'd been on sick leave, and then he was travelling for business.

I had no guarantees that I could even trust the guy—for all he knew I was a violent psychopath—

11:03 am

I called Nelson on my way to the local news-agency, and filled him in on the money situation. He sounded pretty impressed, and promised he'd give the go-ahead to his contact for my passport. I still needed to get a photo to him.

Even from a distance, I recognised the familiar face flapping on the front pages of the newspapers. I crept up to get a closer look and almost burst out laughing. Underneath the head-line 'Bad Kitty', in grainy black and white, was a huge picture of Oriana de la Force's furious face. But that's not what I was laughing at. Her nose had been coloured in black, with what looked like the same thick, indelible ink that had been used on my ankle, and drawn across her cheeks were long, black cat's whiskers! She was caught snarling like a wildcat! It was clear the feline features were Kelvin's handiwork.

'In light of new evidence,' I read, 'Ms de la Force is again facing charges over the kidnapping of Gabbi Ormond, younger sister of the infamous teen fugitive Callum Ormond. Charges brought against de la Force last month were quickly dropped, and she believes the allegations will be dropped again. She has accused her ex-employee of fabricating evidence against her and also for assault after a struggle in which she the police with the forged will. Everything that belonged to your family will be returned to you. You will have your home back, I promise.'

I was always so worried I was going to say something stupid to her, but right now I could see that I had comforted her. She was listening to me and nodding.

'Thanks, Cal,' she whispered. 'I'm really tired. Let's get some sleep.'

9:10 am

As soon as I woke up, I looked down to the floor for Winter. She was gone.

She'd left behind another note, with a couple of dollars on top.

good morning, monkey boy,

had to go, sorry. will buzz u later.
don't forget to check the news—
buy yourself a paper.

x

p.s. and call nelson! oh, and what about
that blair guy? check in with him too!

I find out the truth. I told you, I need to see the wreck of our car. Sligo said that brake failure was the reason for the fatal accident, and I need to see that for myself before I can move on. The guy forged my dad's signature on his will. What else has he done that I don't know about?'

I nodded, and continued listening.

'Look, I know this year has been one crazy, dangerous ride for you, but once it's over,' she said, 'after we've been to Ireland and discovered the truth about the Ormond Singularity—'

I went to interrupt her, but she stopped me short.

'Cal. After all this is over for you, and you've cleared your name, you can go home . . . it may not be your place in Richmond, but you have a family. I can never go *home*. I don't have a home any more. Mum and Dad are gone and Sligo *gave* my parents' house to Murray Durham to pay him off for something. Just gave it away. All I have left is the truth. That's the only thing that will make me feel complete again.'

'Winter,' I said, looking straight into her eyes, 'I will help you, I mean it. I only have one month and a half left to get through, then—if all goes to plan—I will be free to do anything you need me to do. I will help you check the car at the yard, then I will stand by you when you go to

Little Bird

Winter picked up the photo again, and stared at the younger version of herself. 'They always called me Little Bird. I think this was the last time I ever really smiled. Like that, I mean, with all my heart. If I hadn't acted like such a brat, making them take me to the aquarium that day . . .'

'It was raining,' I pleaded. 'Accidents happen on wet roads. Brakes fail. You can't blame yourself,' I reminded her again. 'You can't keep beating yourself up about it. What's the point? You need to let it go.'

'Cal, I can't just *let it go*,' she said firmly. 'Whether I feel guilty or not, it's not over until in the absence of my parents, then when I opened the door, a whole party of people jumped out from hiding, shouting "Surprise!"'

'They'd organised a party for you? They were acting blasé about your birthday because they were keeping the party a surprise?'

Winter closed her eyes. A tear fell down her cheek.

'That's when I burst into tears,' she said. 'The place was decked out with hundreds of pink and purple helium balloons, streamers, and a birthday banner. There was this huge cake on the table. Everyone was staring at me, so confused, wondering where Mum and Dad were.'

'What did you tell them?'

'Nothing. I just stood there, crying. Sligo finally stepped in after me to explain to everyone what had happened. He told them my parents had "perished" in an accident. I just remember a sea of white faces and a wave of murmurs. The house emptied in a blur. Just before Sligo led me out again, a small suitcase in my hand, I picked up the present that sat beside my birthday cake— a small white box, tied with a pink satin bow. I opened it in the car.' Winter held up her heart-shaped locket for me to see. 'It was this. Mum and Dad had it engraved for me. But they never had the chance to see me wear it.'

the needle-like piece of wood out. I flicked it through the window. A small drop of blood appeared on her fingertip.

'It was on the way there,' she continued, seemingly unfazed, 'that Dad lost control of the car. The next thing I knew I was in hospital, wondering where my parents were. I kept watching the doorway, hoping and praying for Mum and Dad to appear, but they never came. Vulkan turned up instead. He walked in and knelt down beside my bed. "Your parents are dead," he said. Four words. Just like that. My family was gone.'

I tightened my arm around my friend, wishing I could erase the memory for her. I hadn't real-ised Sligo had come onto the scene so quickly.

'I didn't even cry,' she said. 'I just felt numb. Completely and utterly numb. Eventually we left the hospital and he took me home. It was just starting to get dark when we pulled up at the house. You remember my house?' she asked me. 'In Dolphin Point—the one we had to break into?'

'I remember,' I nodded.

How could I ever forget?

'Sligo instructed me to go inside, go to my room and put some clothes in a bag. So I walked up to the front door, feeling so dazed and confused around, acting like it was any other, ordinary day. They told me they were just too busy to organise anything for me, and that they'd make it up to me on my eleventh birthday. As I think I mentioned last time to you, I chucked a bit of a tantrum . . .' Her voice trailed off for a moment.

'You don't have to go on,' I said, 'if it's too hard.'

'No, Cal. I've never trusted anyone like I trust you. I really want to get this out. I haven't told you everything,' she said, toying with her heart-shaped locket.

'I'm listening.'

'So,' she continued, picking at a splinter in the floor. 'I chucked this massive tantrum. I thought turning ten was such a big deal, and I couldn't believe they were being so blasé about it. I cried and carried on until they agreed to take me to the aquarium.'

'You wanted to see the seahorses, right?'

'That's right. It was a horrible day, raining and stormy, and they were both supposed to go to a meeting in the afternoon, but I insisted they take me to the aquarium instead.'

I watched as Winter lifted the splinter from the floor. 'Ouch,' she said, suddenly pricking her finger on the sharpest end.

'Careful,' I said, taking her hand and pulling

'Winter, you were adorable,' I couldn't help saying. 'You look so happy.'

'I found the photo in a stash of my old things at Sligo's place,' she explained. 'I'd forgotten this photo existed. Mum was always carrying around her instant camera. I used to love those first few moments after she'd take a picture. She'd always give it to me so I could watch the image slowly come into focus. I thought it was magic.'

'When was it taken?' I asked. I'd have guessed she was about Gabbi's age. 'You can talk to me, Winter,' I said, sensing she was clamming up on me again. 'We're friends, right?'

She nodded. 'You know we're friends. The picture was taken on my tenth birthday,' she said, taking it back from me.

'Your tenth birthday—wasn't that the day of the accident?'

She half smiled as she nodded, as though she was happy I remembered her telling me that detail, but sad casting her mind back to that horrible day.

'It was taken just before we set off for the aquarium,' she said. 'I woke up so excited that morning. I remember ripping off my duvet and literally jumping out of bed. But when I reached the living room, Mum and Dad were pottering

14 NOVEMBER

48 days to go . . .

Treehouse

1:42 am

A cool breeze was drifting in through the tree-house window, gently nudging the flames of the tea-light candles we'd lit. Winter wriggled closer to me. We were sitting on the floor, huddled under a blanket.

'Hey,' she said, softly, 'want to see something funny?'

'Yeah, what ya got?'

After a moment's hesitation, she reached down into her beach bag and dug around, before finally pulling out a small, square photo.

'Here,' she said, passing it to me.

I took it in my hands and carefully peered at the image. In it was a girl with a black bob and fringe, wearing a huge grin, holding up a colourful drawing of a seahorse.

'Sure.' For the last couple of months Winter had really shown her softer side. She definitely wasn't the tough, cold-hearted girl I first thought she was. Far from it. 'As long as you don't mind sleeping on an uneven floor,' I added.

'I can handle that,' she said. 'Just lead the way.'

'Um, yeah,' she said, uncertainly. 'You're off to the treehouse?'

'That's home, right now. How's Lesley Street been since the raid? Have your neighbours been talking?'

'It's been OK. Apparently this one guy who lives on the ground floor contacted the police. He said he'd seen you loitering downstairs.'

'I think I know who that was,' I said, picturing the man in the glasses who'd questioned me about which flat I lived in.

'But don't worry about it; they have no idea about your connection to me. No-one has a clue about you staying in my place. That's the good thing about being hidden away, up on the roof. My guess is that most people forget I'm even up there.'

'That's a relief. I'd hate to get you into trouble.' I adjusted my backpack. 'Thanks heaps for getting this money for me. I'll pay you back one day, I promise.'

'I know you will. Can you do me a favour in the meantime?'

'Course I can. What is it?'

'Can you give me a place to crash tonight?'

'Me? The treehouse?'

'Yeah, do you mind? I don't feel like going back to my empty flat tonight.'

in the moonlight. 'Cool, thanks, I've never worn contacts before.'

'They're super easy to put in.'

'Hey, guess what?' I said. 'Sharkey's going to Ireland too, for a huge family reunion.'

'Really? When?'

'Some time over Christmas.'

'How cool! That means we can all go together!' said Winter. 'It'd be perfect having Nelson with us. He'd know exactly what airport traps we should avoid, and it'd look good for us to be travelling with an "adult". We can pretend he's our teacher or something. Here,' she said, digging into her bag and handing me some wads of cash. 'That's five grand there. That'll cover your passport, and leave you with some extra. Maybe that Ormond Angel is looking out for you—it's about time, considering we only have a few weeks left until the Ormond Singularity dies.'

I really hoped I wouldn't die before it.

11:10 pm

It was getting late, so Winter and I started walking away from the shore. We made our way over the sand and grass in silence, only stopping to speak once we'd reached the road.

'So I guess I'll give you a call soon?' I asked her.

'Careful your bag doesn't get washed away,' I said as I stepped up to join her.

'There'd have to be a tidal wave for me to let that happen. Hey,' she said, moving over to make room for me, 'I have some other really good news for you too. It involves Oriana, but that's all I'm going to tell you right now. You'll find out for yourself soon enough. Just check the news.'

Her cheeky grin told me not to bother trying to find out what she was on about.

'You have no idea how creepy Sligo's bedroom is,' she said, moving on. 'It's all black—even the carpet. I was getting desperate to find the key to his suitcase, frantically feeling around behind all his suits and jackets in the built-in wardrobe. And that's when I finally came across it, taped to the wall behind the suitcase. You'd better let Sharkey know the plan worked, and that he can go ahead and get that guy to start on your fake passport.'

'Definitely. I'll text him a bit later.'

'Here, these are for your passport photo,' she said, handing me a small plastic container. 'Dark brown contact lenses. You should wear them when you get your picture taken—to help you look different.'

I opened the container and looked inside, trying to hold it up so the contents were more visible extract the money, snag the piece of Oriana's scarf on a clothes hook, and get downstairs and into the pool! And here we are,' she said.

Even in the dim light I could see the broad size of her smile.

'Give us a look!' said Boges.

We both leaned in as Winter proudly held the bag open and revealed the cash—wads of one-hundred-dollar notes.

'Ireland, here we come!' said Boges. 'Hey, we could make it a round-the-world trip!'

'Don't get too carried away,' I said.

'Another successful excursion!' said Boges, standing up. 'All right, you two, I'd better get going. I have to start thinking about what story I'm going to tell Mum and Gran to cover the trip. Last year, some of the seniors went to Thailand for a couple of weeks to work with rescued elephants. I guess I could try something like that.'

'Maybe rescued leprechauns?' I suggested.

'Hmm, that could work!' my friend joked. 'Let me know when you want to catch up again.'

10:17 pm

In front of the moon, the sky was purple mauve over the dark sea. Winter sat like a mermaid on the rocks just beyond the reach of the lamps that lit the curving beachfront.

on the forehead out of my mind. Who did he think he was, replacement father of the year? It made me mad.

Impatient, I pulled out my mobile and called her. She picked up almost immediately.

'We're already at the beach. Are you on your way?'

'Almost there,' she said, before hanging up.

'What did she say?' asked Boges. 'What happened?'

Winter suddenly jumped out from the darkness, almost giving us both heart attacks. 'Ten big ones happened!' she said, ducking between us and swinging her arms around our shoulders.

'Ten big ones?' I repeated. 'Ten thousand dollars?'

She nodded and patted her beach bag.

My jaw dropped. Boges's mouth was wide open, too.

'I knew it was in there! I've already counted it,' said Winter. 'I left all the cigar boxes exactly as they were in his bag, minus the money, of course. Unless Vulkan actually needs to open one of the boxes, he won't suspect a thing!'

'But I thought it was locked. How did you get into it?'

'Practically as soon as I hung up from you, I found the key. I just had time to get the bag open, in the back lane. After about two minutes—two painfully slow minutes—we heard a splash in the pool. Both of us exhaled with relief.

8:03 pm

It was a long time before we finally saw Winter leaving Sligo's through the back gate. She'd wrapped her sarong around her like a dress, tied at the neck. The beach towel and bag were slung over her shoulder, and her hair still looked sleek and wet.

She shook her head slowly in our direction, warning us with her eyes. Then we heard footsteps following her. Someone was walking her out. Sligo!

Boges and I crouched down even further, but not before seeing Winter stop and turn to Sligo, who took her in his arms and kissed her on the forehead.

8:43 pm

Once the coast was clear, Boges and I made our way to the beach. Winter had agreed to meet us there as soon as the job was done.

We were sitting on the breakwater, kicking our legs out, both feeling dejected, knowing that Winter had been unable to get into Sligo's suitcase. I couldn't get the image of Sligo kissing her

'I hope she's going to be OK,' I said. 'Sligo will go nuts when he realises his money's missing. Especially when he thinks Oriana's the thief.'

'Maybe he won't even notice for a while,' said Boges. 'Unless he checks the bag every day, it could be weeks before he realises it's been taken.'

It was still hot even though the sun was setting. I took a sip of water out of a drink bottle Boges had brought along.

'Quick,' said Boges, 'look who's coming! You'd better call her.'

The black Subaru, driven by Zombie Two, with Sligo sitting beside him like a toad in a cravat, was cruising along the street. I grabbed my mobile and hit Winter's number.

'They're here,' I hissed, as soon as she picked up. 'Pulling up outside now.'

'He's locked it,' she said, despairing. 'I can't find the key to the suitcase. I don't know where he's put it!'

'Winter,' I said, 'you'll have to forget about it. Just get out of his room and into the pool. You're supposed to be over there for a swim, remember?'

I hung up.

'The suitcase is locked,' I whispered to Boges. He swore under his breath as we waited anxiously

13 NOVEMBER

49 days to go . . .

Boges and I waited in the back lane behind Sligo's place. Sharkey had dropped us off on the street, but he couldn't stick around—he reluctantly admitted to us that he had a 'hot date' to go to!

Winter had disappeared inside the house sometime earlier, wearing a purple sarong over her black bikini, and carrying a towel and the beach bag that concealed the crucial piece of Oriana's leopard-print scarf. Sligo was out right now, so her plan was to get into his room while the place was empty, steal the money from the cigar boxes, stash it into her bag, then dive into the pool just in time for his return home. She'd pretend she'd been splashing around in there all afternoon.

I thought of the last time we'd been at Sligo's, hiding in the pool shed, waiting for Winter's hidden camera to come online, and sweating it out when Bruno almost found us in there.

I decided it was safest to stay put. I pulled the sleeping-bag up over my ears and tried to go back to sleep.

11 NOVEMBER

51 days to go . . .

Treehouse

6:21 am

It was the eleventh of November—the date that had mysteriously appeared across my blog, and the date of Ryan Spencer's birthday. I was huddled in my sleeping-bag, on the floor of the treehouse, woken up by the sound of birds squawking in a nearby tree.

I was pretty sure the date on my blog was from someone trying to alert me to Ryan's existence, but now that the day had come I felt uneasy. What if it was a warning about something completely unrelated to him?

Talking to Ryan would have been a good idea, but I didn't know how to get in touch with him unless I went to his house. I couldn't spring that on him again. Not only that, but I didn't want to risk a trip out. Was I in danger?

I hated the unknown.

fact,' she said, narrowing her eyes, 'it'll be kinda fun to sit there, nodding and smiling, while all the time I have his emergency stash hidden away in my beach bag!'

'Winter,' said Boges, 'you are one fearless chick.'

She winked at him. There was no mistaking the admiration in Boges's voice.

My mobile beeped. It was a text message from Sharkey.

▯ let me know if u want me to go ahead with the passport. as soon as you give me the nod, my friend can get on with it. he'll need the $ and a photo.

'I'll call him back and see if he's keen to help us watch over Sligo's, while you,' I said, turning to Winter, 'sneak into his scram bag and collect.'

I said, 'you'll need to cover yourself. Make it look like a professional break-in. Put him off the scent with a false trail.'

I suddenly thought of something. 'Hey, you have something belonging to Oriana that you could plant. That piece of the leopard-print scarf she used to half-throttle me. It's still at your place, isn't it? You could use that to complicate things.'

Winter's face brightened. 'Love it,' she said. 'Yep, I'll use that, Cal. And leave it at the crime scene. Maybe I could drop a few of those little silver things she's always eating.'

'Sweet,' said Boges. 'They won't be such tight allies after that!'

'I will need your help, though,' she said, looking from Boges to me, 'to make sure of a clean getaway. Just someone to keep an eye on his place, in case something goes wrong.'

'We'll be there,' I said.

'I'll drop by for a swim,' said Winter, 'and invite myself to dinner. I can do that any time. He loves an audience when he's talking about himself. He thinks the rubbish he's telling me—about sponsoring the ballet, about the art he's acquired, about the huge party he wants to host next month—impresses me. I guess I can handle that. I won't have to do it for much longer. In have money in them. *I* don't have to see it to know it's in there.' Winter shrugged. 'I just have to go over there and take it. Sligo owes me a lot of money,' she said. 'The guy stole my inheritance. If we help ourselves to his stash, I would just be getting back a very small fraction of what he's taken from me. As soon as I've returned to his yard and scoped out the wreck of my mum and dad's car, and as soon as we've solved the mystery of the DMO, my relationship with him will be over. I'll be taking my evidence to the police, and then he'll be dead to me. I'll finally be free to move on with the rest of my life.'

'And I'll be right there beside you, when you go to the police,' I said. 'That's a promise.'

'Me too,' said Boges.

She flashed us a grateful smile. I loved the confident way Winter spoke, as if another trip to the car yard was just one minor obstacle standing in the way of the truth about her family. I also loved the way she spoke about the DMO, as if we were about to crack it, any day now.

I just hoped Sligo wouldn't find out prematurely that his ward was spying on him, trying to get evidence on him. If Winter took money from him and he found out, she'd be in real trouble. Underground oil tank trouble.

'If you're going to help yourself to his cash,'

'Cold, hard cash,' said Winter, rubbing her fingers together in front of our faces.

I recalled how Sligo had handed Rathbone a cigar case last month, back at the banquet. Was he paying him off for something?

'Have you actually seen this cold, hard cash?' I asked Winter.

The look on her face instantly told me she hadn't.

'Look, I know it's in there. I've seen him hand the cases over to people in the past, and I know Sligo's passing around more than just cigars. I caught a glimpse inside the scram bag yesterday and he has a row of these boxes stacked along one side of the suitcase. He doesn't even like smoking cigars! Trust me, they're lined with money.'

'Dangerous,' I warned. 'You said he's been acting funny—more paranoid. What were you doing over there, snooping in his room?'

'I wanted to confirm my theory on the money in the cases, but I ran out of time. I took lunch over to him, then snuck into his room while he was taking a call. I saw the cigar boxes in the bag, but I freaked out thinking he was about to walk in on me, so I didn't get any further than that.'

'So it's just a theory?' Boges asked.

'I'll say it again for you. I know the boxes

Winter pulled her hair back and twisted it around, then let it fall again before answering us. 'Sligo—'

'Oh, no, not him,' Boges interrupted. 'I don't like any sentence that starts with that name.'

Hands on hips, Winter snapped back. 'Do you guys want to know, or not?'

'You know we do,' I said, elbowing Boges. 'Go on.'

'*Sligo* keeps a packed suitcase in the back of his wardrobe. I overheard him call it his "scram bag". I'm not supposed to know about it, of course, but as you guys know, I make it my business to find out everything that goes on in Vulkan Sligo's place.'

'Scram bag?' I asked, repeating her phrase.

She nodded. 'His emergency suitcase. Already packed. Ready to scram. So he can grab it and get out of the country at a moment's notice. Everything's there—passport, travel documents, clothes, toothbrush, cologne . . . and *cigar boxes*.'

'Cigar boxes?' I asked. 'I don't get it. Cigars aren't worth *that* much, are they?'

I turned to Boges, but he looked as confused as me.

'It's not the cigars that I'm interested in,' said Winter, 'it's what else is inside the cigar boxes!'

'Money?'

I slumped against the wall, hot and exhausted with everything.

'Airfares, accommodation expenses,' Boges continued. 'Even if we live in youth hostels we'll still need to find more money. I'll talk to my uncle. He might have some ideas about cheap travel.'

That idea didn't help lift my gloomy mood.

Suddenly, I brightened up. 'Rathbone's garden! We can dig up his money chest!'

'Whoa, dude,' said Boges. 'As if he would have left that stash there.'

'Yeah, whoa, dude,' repeated Winter. 'He definitely would have moved that and hidden it somewhere else by now.'

They were both right. Unlucky for me.

'You won't find money buried in Rathbone's garden any more,' said Winter hesitantly, 'but I do know another place where you'll find a lot of money.'

'Where?' I asked.

'I know where there's money, too,' said Boges, pointing down to Zürich Bank in the distance. 'There's all we need and more, just over there.'

Winter rolled her eyes. 'I'm talking serious money I can actually get my hands on. Straight away, if necessary.'

'Tell us,' I urged.

and sixty-two bucks short,' said Boges. 'And forty-five cents. Here, I think I can chip in the forty-five cents,' he said, digging into his pocket. He handed me a fifty-cent piece. 'Keep the change.'

'Boges,' I said, 'this is serious.'

We looked up as Winter approached us from the stairs. The wind was whipping her dark hair across her face, and big sunglasses hid her eyes. Lately she always seemed to be wearing jeans and T-shirts, instead of the crazy skirts and shawls I first saw her in. Today she wore dark jeans, white sneakers and a red and white striped shirt, reminding me of a peppermint candy cane.

'My passport's sorted,' she said, with a smile.

'Mine, too,' said Boges.

'I'm excited,' she said, nudging Boges and me with her shoulders. 'So when are we going to Ireland?'

Then she saw my face.

'Problem?' she asked.

'No passport. No Ireland.'

'You have to get one. You can't give up like that.'

'Who said I'm giving up? I can *get* a passport, but it's going to cost me. Somehow, I need to find almost four thousand dollars.'

'Plus you need money for flights, and it'll cost money once you get to Ireland,' Boges said.

'I know, thanks for the reminder,' I groaned.

it and get back to me,' he said before hanging up.

4:18 pm

After the Lesley Street raid that almost trapped me, there was no way I was going to use Winter's flat as a meeting place. I called my friends and asked them to meet me at the top of the clock tower instead. I liked this place as a rendezvous point, with its unbeatable aerial view of the city, although I knew I'd be in big trouble if I found a SWAT team ascending the stairs—there weren't any rooftops *this* high I could jump to as an escape.

'Boges,' I said, as soon as he arrived, breathless from running up the stairs. 'I have a big problem. Sharkey knows a really good forger—' I began.

'That's not a problem, that's a good thing,' he said.

'Wait until you hear his price,' I continued. 'Five grand.'

Boges's hands flew to his head. The nervous scratching began.

'Sharkey scored one thousand for the leftover gold I had, and I have one hundred and thirty-seven dollars, fifty-five cents in my pocket.'

'That leaves you three thousand, eight hundred

9 NOVEMBER

53 days to go . . .

Treehouse

2:16 pm

Three days up a tree later, I was relieved when
Sharkey called me with some news.

'I scored one thousand for the gold,' he said.
'I tried to get more but that was the best I could
do.'

'Thanks, Sharkey. That's heaps better than
what I got for the other half.'

'Happy to help. Now listen, I'm tracking down
a very good forger I know, who owes me a favour
or two. But you'll need at least another four
grand. He doesn't work for anything under five.'

'Four grand!' I nearly choked as the impossible words came out of my mouth. 'He wants
another four grand? I need to have enough cash
for flights, too. How am I supposed to make all
this happen?'

'Cal, I don't have all the solutions. Think about

'I don't know a great deal about gold value, but I'm pretty certain you have it covered.'

'Cool. By the way, do the names Deep Water, Double Trouble and The Little Prince mean anything to you?' I asked, hoping that the ex-detective might recognise the criminal nicknames.

Nelson Sharkey frowned, then shook his head. 'No. Where'd you hear them?'

'I saw them listed with the names of some other crims,' I said. 'I thought maybe you'd have heard of them.'

'No, not familiar, I'm afraid.'

'If I get the money—' I started to say.

'How are you going to do that, Cal?' he said sternly, in a way that my dad would've spoken to me if I'd just suggested something he thought was going to put me in danger. 'I think a trip to Ireland would be good, but not if you have to do something crazy to get the money for it.'

'I'm not about to go and hold up a bank,' I said with a half-smirk. 'There's no need, when I already have this,' I said, reaching into my pocket for the pouch of remaining gold nuggets.

Nelson Sharkey whistled when he took the pouch from me and peered inside at the gleaming gold. 'Where the heck did you get this?'

'Remember how I told you about the two old Dingo Bones Valley prospectors? One of them tried to tie me up—wanted to hand me over to the cops for the reward money—and in the struggle I pocketed some of *his* bounty . . . kinda like a souvenir.'

'Right, a souvenir,' said Sharkey, tipping some of the gold into his palm.

'Do you think you could trade it in for me?' I pictured the suspicious gold trader who'd given me the money for the first half of my stash. I couldn't risk trying to cash it in with him again. 'That should be enough to cover the passport, right?'

For a moment I wished things were different for him. The way he'd contacted me, offering me his help, made it obvious he still wanted to be working for justice. Even if it was in an unofficial way. I could tell he really missed the job, but he refused to admit it. I recalled how he'd told me about his former boss betraying him, and setting him up, which led to the loss of his badge. He'd also mentioned losing touch with his kids because of it. Maybe he reached out to me because he had a kid of his own that was my age. A kid who he couldn't talk to.

I was too afraid to ask him about his family. 'Will you help me get a fake passport?' I asked him, instead.

'Where do you think we're going to get the money from?' He leaned towards me. 'I told you, I don't have a lot of money. Definitely not that kind of money. And I can't imagine you have hundreds of dollars in *your* pockets.'

I didn't have hundreds of dollars in my pockets, but I had something just as good. 'If money wasn't a problem, would you be able to arrange the passport for me?' I asked.

'Of course I could. Anything's possible in this city. All you need is the right connections *and* the right amount of money in your wallet.' He leaned back in his seat, and fiddled with the lid of his drink bottle.

who originated from this place called Roscommon, in Ireland, are meeting up there over Christmas for a twenty-five-year reunion. We're expecting nearly a thousand people to descend on the place, from all over the world—America, England, Australia.' His face became serious. 'I guess you want to go to Ireland to find out more about your dad's final activities?'

'That's right,' I said, nodding.

'Probably a good idea,' he said. 'It will be a heck of a struggle to get you out of the country, but there's not much else you can do here right now. The answers you've been looking for—if they exist—will most likely be found there. In my opinion.'

Slowly I took in what Sharkey was saying. I was lucky to have someone like him to give me advice.

'So you'll go to Ireland, you'll track down whatever this Ormond Singularity thing is that you told me about, you'll claim the reward—or whatever it is—and then you can come back and clear your name. Is that your plan?'

'That's the plan. I bet you were a great detective in your day,' I said. 'Don't you ever want to get back into it?'

Nelson grunted, and brushed the idea away with a flick of his hands. 'Too corrupt,' he said, bitterly.

6 NOVEMBER

56 days to go . . .

Fit For Life

5:55 pm

I met the ex-detective at the gym. I noticed how his watchful eyes constantly scanned the street outside as he listened to what I had to say.

'Cal, of course it's do-able,' Sharkey said, 'but do you have any idea how much a false passport costs?'

'I'm sure they're not cheap,' I said. 'I was hoping you could tell me and help me arrange one.'

'Where do you want to go?'

'Ireland,' I said.

'Ireland? You're going to Ireland?' Sharkey looked surprised.

'Where else would I want to go?' I asked. 'Disneyland?'

'No, it's just a coincidence,' he said, laughing. 'I'm about to head off there myself, to a family reunion. My family's Irish, and all the Sharkeys

'I'd better get going—big day at school tomorrow. Maybe you should give Nelson Sharkey a call. See if he can help you out with a passport.'

that the grass had grown right over it. I cautiously flashed my torch around.

Five years ago, I'd been able to stand up. Now, I had to bend down slightly to fit inside.

'Look,' said Boges, 'even the carpet squares are still here. And the curtains. Not too shabby, either.' He straightened some of the carpet on the uneven timber floor with his foot as he spoke. 'And I added these,' he said, pulling a couple of red cushions out from behind him on the bench. 'There's some food in that box, too.'

I opened the lid on the old wooden toy box in the corner. Inside were some cans of tuna, baked beans, nuts, crisps and a loaf of bread.

'You should be pretty comfortable here for a while, at least until something better becomes available. There's plenty of bushy cover and there's a tap just a few metres away that looks pretty unused. The only major downside is that there's no power source for charging your phone in here, but I checked out the shed—it's up closer to the house—and found a power point. You could probably sneak up there and use it at night, when you really need to.'

'Yeah, this is cool,' I said, pushing my backpack into the toy box with the food. 'It doesn't have a home cinema, but it'll do. Thanks, Boges.'

My friend laughed before getting up to leave.

Rathbone doesn't know.' I leaned against the railing. 'The days are running out. We just have to plan our trip to Ireland and hope we luck onto the Jewel and the Riddle before it's time to leave. I still have a gold stash, remember. Somehow I'll use it to get a passport.'

We sat together in gloomy silence until Boges whacked me on the knee, getting to his feet. 'I have things to do at home. Come on, let's get going. The home of your ancestors awaits you.'

'My ancestors?'

Boges jumped around like a gorilla, grunting and beating his chest.

'You're talking about the treehouse, right?'

'Correct. I made a few adjustments to it this morning, in preparation for your visit. Follow me.'

Treehouse

8:32 pm

'So, what you think?' Boges asked, making himself comfortable on the treehouse bench. We'd climbed up the new rope he'd attached to the rear of the tree, and snuck in through the window in the back. Here, hidden among the dense foliage, and far away from Luke Lovett's house, the treehouse snuggled secretly, like a forgotten toy that had been resting on the lawn so long down to me, telling me to wait for her by the door.'

'Unreal,' I said, in awe again of Winter. She'd helped us out too many times to count. Risked her safety and her life. I owed her. Big time.

'So did she get the door open?'

'Yep, that took a while too, but she cleared the grass and cut the lock off with bolt cutters she found in the gardener's shed. It felt good to be back on ground level.'

7:54 pm

The air was still warm and smelled of salt and the sea, reminding me of the night I'd spent struggling on the upturned boat, fighting off the sharks way back in January. In spite of everything that had happened, all our efforts, the way we'd solved most of the drawings, we were still pretty clueless.

'It's November,' I said to Boges. 'The Ormond Singularity runs out next month. We don't even have the Riddle or the Jewel.' I sat down on the stone steps leading onto the beach. 'We have to get to Ireland somehow, and talk to the Keeper of Rare Books. Copies and photos will have to do.'

'He told you he had to see the original Ormond Riddle manuscript.'

'Boges, we don't even know who has it. Even

dislodge it from its hinges. It wouldn't move. I almost started shouting for help, before Winter pounced on me and covered my mouth to stop me. So she wanders off into the darkness and I'm standing there thinking it's gonna be death by starvation, when I realise Winter's climbing up on an upturned rubbish bin, and pulling herself back into the laundry chute!'

'What?'

'She calls out to me, "Don't just stand there staring, come and give me a boost!"'

'That girl thinks she can do anything,' I said, shaking my head, thinking of Winter and her determination to do even the most impossible things. 'How long did she last up there?'

'Dude,' said Boges, before pausing. 'It took her a while, but *she made it*.'

'She made it? But you said the drop was about six floors! How could she have climbed back up? It was a laundry chute—she wouldn't have had anything to grab onto!'

'I don't know, but that chick is amazing. Seriously. I helped her up and she just kinda dug her boots and her back into the walls of the chute, and pushed herself up, centimetre by centimetre. A few times she slipped a bit and lost some ground, but before I knew it the tunnel was clear and she was standing at the top and shouting floor, picking leaves and spider webs out of her hair, grinning at me like a hyena.'

'One of history's great escapes,' I said.

'That was only the beginning. We weren't out of trouble yet,' he said, eyes as wide as saucers, making me glad I already knew the story had a happy ending. 'So there we were in this black hole in the basement of the building, where no foot has trod for about half a century, only to find that the door's locked. It wouldn't budge.'

'Weren't you worried the cops were going to storm in and find you?'

'*I was.*'

'What about Winter? If the cops found her, while searching for me, and decided to question her, Sligo would find out she'd been helping me and he'd want to kill her.'

'I know, but Winter reckoned the entrance to the basement was completely overgrown with weeds. The door was outside the building, on the ground near the bins. It's one of those trapdoor types. You know that spot?'

'Yeah,' I said, picturing the grassy area he was talking about. 'I think so.'

'She was sure they wouldn't know the basement existed. We waited about an hour or so for the heat to die down outside before we started kicking up at the basement door, trying to back to this metal box thing, kicked the lid off with her boots, then stepped inside and began lowering herself into it.'

'Huh?'

'It was an old laundry chute! She stopped for a second to tell me that I'd better jump in after her if I wanted to get away, then she let go of the sides and disappeared. She was gone in a flash! I heard a kind of whooshing noise and then a bit of an echoing thud a few seconds later!'

I tried imagining the scene.

'Did you do it? Did you follow her? How far was the drop?'

'It must have been over six floors! I didn't want to do it, but by this time,' Boges continued, 'those big mean guys with helmets and riot sticks were spilling over onto the roof. I didn't have any choice. I heaved myself up, sucked in my stomach, and jumped in just like Winter had.'

Boges paused, shaking his head in disbelief. He put his hand gingerly on the left side of his forehead where I could see a bruise.

'Dude, what a ride! I was free-falling for ages. I banged my head, I scraped my sides and tumbled out onto this pile of dusty, filthy old rags that might have been clothes when Captain Cook was a kid. Then when I looked up, I could see Winter a couple of metres away. She was sprawled on the

'I don't know, dude. Someone wanted you to know about it.'

'It doesn't make sense. So tell me,' I said, changing the subject, 'how did you guys get away?'

'Man, it's quite a story. How about I meet you on the beach later on—behind the old Seagull Café—and tell you all about it then?'

7:35 pm

The rows of breakers, dim white moving lines rolling towards the sand, were lit by the tall lamp posts along the beachfront.

Boges and I were hidden in the shadows behind the closed and deserted café. Only a few people were strolling along the beach as Boges proceeded to describe to me how he and Winter had evaded the massive police search.

'We were totally snookered. There was no way either of us was going to follow your lead and leap across buildings, but the cops were swarming up the stairs. We rushed back into the flat and started gathering up the drawings, notes—anything potentially incriminating—then Winter grabbed onto my hand and wrenched me back outside. I was like, "What are you doing? You're leading us to them!" and she was like, "Stop talking and follow me!" Then she dragged me out the

3 NOVEMBER

59 days to go . . .

10:10 am

'Dude, we were freaking out when you took that jump!' said Boges.

'*I* was freaking out,' I said. 'I almost didn't make it!' I'd just called him from the beach—where I'd slept overnight—and I'd spent the last fifteen minutes telling him about how I got away and found myself facing Ryan Spencer's mum in her kitchen. 'So guess when Ryan's birthday is?'

'The same as yours?' Boges asked, intrigued.

'Nope. One more guess.'

There was only a second's hesitation. 'Eleventh of November?'

'Eleventh of November.'

'Are you serious?'

'Deadly. Straight away I drilled him on hacking my blog—but he seriously had no idea what I was talking about. Surely the dates are connected, but why would someone go to that length to cover my blog with it?'

134

before, but I think her opinion will change now that she's seen us side-by-side.'

'We'll talk some other time,' I called as I snuck out of the door.

Ryan saw me looking at it and pointed to the photo on the pass. 'See?' he said. 'That's why they keep pulling me over. I don't know why, but we're unbelievably alike.'

It wasn't his photo I was staring at.

'Is that your birthday?' I asked, amazed at the date on his pass.

'Sure it is. The eleventh of November. Why? Don't tell me it's the same as yours?'

For a moment, I was speechless. It was the repeated date from my blog! *11 November!*

'No, I was born in July,' I said, before bluntly asking, 'Did you hack my blog?'

'What?' His face showed complete surprise. 'What are you talking about?' he asked. 'I've never hacked anybody's blog. Wouldn't know how!'

Ryan's mum moved her head from side to side and started murmuring.

'Cal, I think you'd better go before she comes around. I don't think she's ready for this just yet,' he said, gesturing from his face to mine.

I stood up. 'I'm sorry,' I said, wondering how Ryan was going to explain me to his mum. 'I hope she's OK.'

'Don't worry, she'll be fine. She's never really admitted to seeing the similarities between us ducked up a sneaky alley, lost them, then just walked home.'

'But how come you helped me?' I asked. 'Every other time I've seen you, you've run from me.'

He was looking hard into my eyes. Was he seeing what I was seeing? It was like looking into a mirror—my own bewildered eyes staring back at me.

'I read through your blog a little while ago. I'm not convinced you're a bad guy. But why do *you* keep running?' he asked. 'Why don't you just hand yourself in and prove that you're innocent?'

'There's too much at stake right now. I can't take the risk of being locked up—I have too much to do that depends on my freedom. And it's not just the police who are after me . . .'

'It's been hard for me too, looking like you,' said Ryan as he wetted the tea towel and wiped at his mum's brow once more. 'Everywhere I go the cops hassle me. Even my neighbours nearly handed me in last week, until my mum intervened and told them they were crazy. That's why I spray the "No Psycho" tag all over the walls of the city. I'm sick of people thinking I'm you—it's been going on for almost a year now.'

I took a look at the bus pass hanging from his belt. It looked brand new—a replacement for the one I'd stolen through his open window.

just stared at us, gaping at us wordlessly, looking from Ryan to me, then back again.

Then, her eyes rolled back into her head and her knees folded under her. In a slow and graceful movement, she collapsed onto the tiled floor, completely passed out.

'Mum!' cried Ryan, dumping the groceries and rushing to her side. 'Quick, get some water,' he said to me.

I grabbed a glass off the counter and filled it at the sink. I squatted down to join him on the ground, on the other side of Mrs Spencer's body. Ryan dabbed a tea towel into the water and wiped his mum's brow.

I quickly looked her over, checking her pulse and breathing.

'She just fainted from shock,' I reassured Ryan. 'She'll be OK in a moment. I didn't mean to scare her—I just thought I'd come up and see if you were here.'

Ryan and I lifted his mum into a sitting position, leaning her up against the cupboards.

'Thanks for your help the other night,' I said. 'I couldn't have escaped without you.'

'You don't have to thank me,' Ryan said, as his mum stirred slightly. 'I gave them a run for their money—led them on for about fifteen kilometres, I reckon. Then I chucked your blazer, made the decision for me. I hurried through the entrance, behind the ladies, just as the doors were closing.

I ducked down, unnoticed, as the pair slowly trundled up the stairs. I took a few deep breaths and wondered whether taking this diversion was such a good idea.

As soon as the stairs were clear, I hurried up them, stopping outside Ryan's door. It was slightly ajar, and a delicious smell was wafting out of the kitchen and into the stairwell. I gave it a gentle push and stepped inside.

'That was quick,' said a woman, leaning over the kitchen bench. She stood with her back to me near the sink, beating something in a large blue and white bowl. Without turning around, she spoke again. 'Ryan, can you please hand me the milk, and then put everything else in the fridge?'

I froze. I didn't know what to do!

'Ryan?' she repeated, back still turned.

I swung around as someone else barged in through the door behind me, carrying a bag of groceries.

Ryan Spencer!

At that moment, the woman in the kitchen casually turned around. She was about to say something, but then she saw the two of us standing together near the door. For a few seconds she floor. I'd jumped from one building to another, so dropping down one floor wasn't about to stop me!

I landed hard, and looked around. Not too far away, sirens wailed. I could hear a helicopter overhead and realised that the police search would be fanning out all over this area.

My heart was racing from the terrifying leap I'd just pulled off. Fuelled with the adrenaline of both terror and elation, my running speed hit a high-octane gear. All I could think of was getting as far away from the area as fast as I could.

I hurried on automatic, head down, avoiding eye contact, yet with every cell of my being alert to the slightest hint of danger. I hurried across roads, turned corners, ran up long streets and alleys. I didn't care where I was going, just as long as I was getting away.

7:10 pm

When I found myself hurrying past a familiar building, I slowed down to glance up—I was running past Ryan Spencer's apartment block! I stopped in my tracks and turned back to the entrance, noticing a pair of elderly women strolling through the doors with shopping bags. Should I follow them in? I wondered.

A cop car suddenly cruising down the road

I kicked my legs against the bricks and swung towards the pipe. I missed it.

I kicked out again.

This time I swung out further, and clamped down on the pipe with both of my feet. As soon as I had a good foothold, I slid my hands along the gutter until they were directly above me, then I pushed and hauled myself up and onto the roof.

I looked up at Winter's building. I could see nothing, but I could hear the commotion as the SWAT team finally poured out onto the roof. I hoped like crazy that my friends had somehow escaped in time. If the cops discovered Boges and Winter's connection to me, they'd both be in very serious trouble. I didn't want to think about Sligo finding out.

6:34 pm

Keeping low, I hurried over to the furthest side of the roof, relieved to see that the next building joined the one I was on. I dropped down onto its roof, and kept running, past the air-conditioner housing and other pipes and fittings.

This building had a small access ladder curving over the edge of its roof. I climbed over and started my way down.

The ladder stopped just short of the first

You can't let the cops find you either! Don't worry about me, get away while you can!'

Summoning every ounce of strength and will-power, I backed away from the edge until I was almost at the opposite side of the flat roof. Then I took off, running straight for the wall, as fast as I could!

I stepped up on a plant box with my left leg, then stepped up on the roof edge with my right, then launched myself into the air, yelling, clawing myself further and further along.

I wasn't going fast enough! The roof of the other building was too far—I wasn't going to make it!

Gravity took hold and my body started free-falling. All I could see was the gutter—my only hope. I reached out desperately for it.

Behind me I heard Winter scream.

Incredibly, my fingers caught the gutter and my body swung down and slammed against the wall of the building. I looked up, legs dangling, and saw the metal already bending and buckling under my weight. I looked down and nearly puked on seeing how high I was.

'Cal! The pipe!' shouted Winter. 'Use it to help you get up!'

I spotted the pipe on my right.

'Just get away before *you're* caught!' I yelled back through gritted teeth.

there—the next building was a street's width away.

I raced back to the other side again. This was the only possibility. A big jump. From this roof to the roof of the lower building alongside.

'You're not thinking of jumping across there!' cried Winter, running over and grabbing my arm. 'Cal, it's too dangerous! That gap's too big! You'll never make it!'

Boges bolted to my side.

'Dude, don't do it! You need to stay alive more than you need to get away from the cops!'

He was probably right, but I'd already made my decision.

Winter gasped as I leaned over the parapet to get a better look. Carefully, I stood up on the plant box in front of it. Between the buildings was a massive drop. If I missed, I'd end up down there, splattered all over the pavement.

'Dude, don't do it. Please,' begged Boges.

'Cal,' Winter pleaded. 'We'll think of something else. There must be somewhere you can hide. Don't try this. It's too dangerous. You'll be killed.'

Now I could hear the voices of the cops coming up the fire-escape.

'If they catch me now, I'll never get to the bottom of the Ormond Singularity. Anyway, it's just as important that you two get out of here!

The building was surrounded!

I raced back inside Winter's flat.

'The place is surrounded with cops! They're crawling in the street in front of this place and there's a whole gang of them at the bottom of the fire-escape in the backyard.'

Winter ran out to the parapet overlooking the backyard. She spun around, her hand over her mouth. 'Oh my God! They're about to come up!'

'They must have followed you!' I said, turning to Boges.

'Why me, dude? They might have followed *you*!'

'Shut up, you two!' Winter yelled. 'This is no time to be arguing. Cal! You have to get out of here!'

'I'd have to be able to fly!' I said. 'The building's surrounded!'

I could practically hear the cops out front running up the stairs, taking them two at a time up to the top of the building.

There was no escaping through the back way or the front. I ran to the right side of the building. About three metres lower than the flat roof I was standing on was the roof of another block of flats with a three-metre gap between the buildings. Could I jump that?

I raced to the other side. There was no hope

'OK, well I'll sort this out. I'll do what I can to clean it up. I don't know how, just yet, but I'll make it all nice again. This could just be some kind of spam. Some kind of advertising.'

'I'm not so sure,' said Winter. 'I think it's a warning. This blog has more protection than most, right?'

'Right,' answered Boges.

'Your average spammer can't do that.'

Something alerted me in the silence that followed her words. All of a sudden, the building was too quiet.

'Something's wrong,' I said, jumping up.

'What?' Winter's shadowed eyes, dark with concern, shot over to the windows. Carefully, I opened the door and looked outside.

'What is it, Cal?'

Danger! Every instinct in my body was warning me! I shouldn't have risked hanging around at Winter's flat again.

I looked outside again. The hot expanse of the flat roof was empty.

'Police siren!' I hissed. I ran outside and looked way down to the street below.

I jumped back in horror at what I saw!

I rushed to the rear side of the building where the fire-escape steps descended to the backyard. Again, I recoiled in shock.

'Is something stuck?' I said. 'What's with that text?'

'It's nothing to do with my machine,' said Boges, looking flustered and hitting combinations of keys. 'It's just doing it by itself! Someone's hacked your blog!'

'Hacked my blog? But how?'

'I don't know!' said Boges.

'What's going to happen on the eleventh of November?' asked Winter.

The three of us looked at each other. We were all blank.

'That date doesn't mean anything to any of us?' I asked.

'No, dude.'

Winter shook her head. 'Nothing.'

'It has to mean something for someone to have hacked my blog to make it known,' I said. 'But is it a warning or a threat?'

Nobody answered.

'Boges, can we still post a message?' I asked.

Boges spread his hands out helplessly. 'It won't let me do anything. It's completely frozen. I'm going to have to close it down.'

With a few deft keystrokes, Boges shut down the page. He looked up at me. 'Think hard. Are you sure you have no idea what that date might mean?'

I shook my head. 'Seriously no idea.'

11 NOVEMBER 11 NOVEMBER 11 NOVEMBER 11 NOVEMBER 11 N
OVEMBER 11 NOVEMBER 11 NOVEMBER 11 NOVEMBER 11 NOVE
MBER 11 NOVEMBER 11 NOVEMBER 11 NOVEMBER 11 NOVEMB
ER 11 NOVEMBER 11 NOVEMBER 11 NOVEMBER 11 NOVEMBER
11 NOVEMBER 11 NOVEMBER 11 NOVEMBER 11 NOVEMBER 11 N
OVEMBER 11 NOVEMBER 11 NOVEMBER 11 NOVEMBER 11 NOVE
MBER 11 NOVEMBER 11 NOVEMBER 11 NOVEMBER 11 NOVEMB
ER 11 NOVEMBER 11 NOVEMBER 11 NOVEMBER 11 NOVEMBER
11 NOVEMBER 11 NOVEMBER 11 NOVEMBER 11 NOVEMBER 11 N
OVEMBER 11 NOVEMBER 11 NOVEMBER 11 NOVEMBER 11 NOVE
MBER 11 NOVEMBER 11 NOVEMBER 11 NOVEMBER 11 NOVEMB
ER 11 NOVEMBER 11 NOVEMBER 11 NOVEMBER 11 NOVEMBER
11 NOVEMBER 11 NOVEMBER 11 NOVEMBER 11 NOVEMBER 11 N
OVEMBER 11 NOVEMBER 11 NOVEMBER 11 NOVEMBER 11 NOVE
MBER 11 NOVEMBER 11 NOVEMBER 11 NOVEMBER 11 NOVEMB
ER 11 NOVEMBER 11 NOVEMBER 11 NOVEMBER 11 NOVEMBER
11 NOVEMBER 11 NOVEMBER 11 NOVEMBER 11 NOVEMBER 11 N
OVEMBER 11 NOVEMBER 11 NOVEMBER 11 NOVEMBER 11 NOVE
MBER 11 NOVEMBER 11 NOVEMBER 11 NOVEMBER 11 NOVEMB
ER 11 NOVEMBER 11 NOVEMBER 11 NOVEMBER 11 NOVEMBER
11 NOVEMBER 11 NOVEMBER 11 NOVEMBER 11 NOVEMBER 11 N
OVEMBER 11 NOVEMBER 11 NOVEMBER 11 NOVEMBER 11 NOVE
MBER 11 NOVEMBER 11 NOVEMBER 11 NOVEMBER 11 NOVEMB
ER 11 NOVEMBER 11 NOVEMBER 11 NOVEMBER 11 NOVEMBER
11 NOVEMBER 11 NOVEMBER 11 NOVEMBER 11 NOVEMBER 11 N
OVEMBER 11 NOVEMBER 11 NOVEMBER 11 NOVEMBER 11 NOVE
MBER 11 NOVEMBER 11 NOVEMBER 11 NOVEMBER 11 NOVEMB
ER 11 NOVEMBER 11 NOVEMBER 11 NOVEMBER 11 NOVEMBER
11 NOVEMBER 11 NOVEMBER 11 NOVEMBER 11 NOVEMBER 11 N
OVEMBER 11 NOVEMBER 11 NOVEMBER 11 NOVEMBER 11 NOVE
MBER 11 NOVEMBER 11 NOVEMBER 11 NOVEMBER 11 NOVEMB
ER 11 NOVEMBER 11 NOVEMBER 11 NOVEMBER 11 NOVEMBER
11 NOVEMBER 11 NOVEMBER 11 NOVEMBER 11 NOVEMBER 11 N

and who's going to believe him against a hotshot lawyer?'

'Unless he does have some physical evidence against her,' I said. 'Like DNA or video footage showing her with Gabbi.'

'Who knows,' said Boges. 'Hey, want to write anything on your blog while I have my laptop out?'

'I guess . . . It's been a while,' I grunted. I had a bad feeling. I wasn't sure why. Maybe Winter's paranoia had rubbed off on me. While waiting for Boges to access my blog, I stood up and went to the window, lifting the curtain and looking outside.

Boges gasped.

I let the curtain fall and turned back. 'What is it?'

My stomach started churning when I saw the alarmed expression on Boges's face as he stared at the screen.

'What's that?' cried Winter, who'd crept behind him to peer over his shoulder at the screen.

'What's *what*?' I asked, nervously approaching the laptop.

Something seriously weird was happening. Pages and pages of repeated numbers and words were scrolling over the screen. I focused my eyes to try and catch what it said.

to describe how I feel. Sligo's just extremely edgy lately. Everything that went on at his banquet has really spooked him. He's always been paranoid, but now . . .'

'Winter,' I said, holding her hand. 'Just promise me you'll be really, really careful in future. I'm here for you. Always.'

Winter squeezed my hand.

'Don't rush anything, OK?' I said. 'If you can hold out just a little bit longer, we'll both be able to help you sort everything out.'

'That's right,' added Boges. 'We're *both* here for you. Sligo is one dangerous dude. I really think you should let me design something for you—something in the line of personal self-defence.'

'Nothing that requires detonation,' I said, hastily.

'I was thinking some kind of skunk gas, actually. It could be—'

'Forget it!' Winter interrupted.

Something suddenly popped into my head. 'Kelvin dobbed Oriana in over Gabbi's kidnapping, right? Remember the footage we saw of her going ballistic on TV? Why is she still around?'

'Allegations are one thing,' said Boges. 'Getting enough evidence against someone is a different matter. The police need evidence. At the moment, it's just Kelvin's word against Oriana's—

Cal, you have the *combined* forces of the king and queen of the underworld after you.'

It felt like Sligo and Oriana had been after me forever—and that had made my life tough enough—but now they were working together?

'And there's something else,' said Winter, looking away. 'I'm not exactly sure, but I feel like something's up with Sligo. I mean, something's up in the way he's acting with me. He looks at me differently, and I'm scared that he's on to me, that he suspects something.'

'What makes you say that?' asked Boges.

'A couple of times I've looked up to find him scrutinising me. Then he looks away really fast, pretending he wasn't doing it. Maybe he's seen me snooping in his office or in the car yard. I think I know all the security cameras to avoid, but maybe there are hidden ones that I don't know about. I might be imagining the whole thing, you know, because I feel so guilty when I'm snooping through Sligo's stuff.'

'Guilty?' I asked. 'What do you have to feel guilty about? He forged your dad's will, remember? And you would never have found that out without your snooping.'

'I know, I know,' she said. 'How could I forget? It hasn't left my mind since I found his phoney signature. I don't think "guilty" is the right word at the library lately,' Winter began, 'I've been completely distracted by this list, trying to work out who the names could belong to. But still, I haven't really figured out anything. Only Rathbone knows who they are—he's the one who came up with them. And obviously he was frustrated with getting nowhere, if you found the list in the bin.'

She hesitated, as if she were about to say something more, but then shook her head. Her deep, dark eyes looked steadily into mine, and then she turned away. 'We're up against more than we bargained for. Maybe Nelson can help us.'

Winter looked awkwardly at Boges and then at me.

Boges squirmed uncomfortably. 'If you'd like me to leave or something,' he said, 'I can.'

'No, Boges,' she said. 'You should hear this, too.' She turned to me. 'Cal, the reason I needed to talk to you wasn't just because of those nicknames. Sligo called me, asking me for help.'

'What kind of help?' I blurted out.

'He thinks that because you and I are similar ages, I might have heard something, somehow. As far as I can tell he's more convinced than ever that you're the one holding the Riddle and the Jewel, and now he has Oriana convinced too.

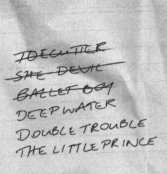

'And get this,' Winter said, 'part of the story involves the interpretation of drawings, and—' she paused for effect, looking hard at me, '—a boy and a rose. Remind you of anything?'

'Freaky,' I said, recalling Dad's drawing of exactly that. The three of us looked at each other.

'Rathbone must know a lot about my dad's drawings and how important they are for decoding the Ormond Singularity,' I said, 'to pick a nickname like that.'

'All the hours I've spent with Miss Sparks

transmitter. I tore the rubbery piece out of my shoe then tossed it into the bin. The transmitter fitted perfectly in the gap I'd created.

'Cool,' said Boges. 'Now use some of this to tape it down.'

He handed me some electrical tape. As smoothly as I could, I taped the beacon down, replaced the inner sole, then put my trainer back on and stood up, walking around the small room.

'It just feels like I have a coin stuck in my shoe.'

'You'll get used to it,' said Boges.

'Thanks, Boges. This is cool. Hopefully I won't actually have to use it.'

'So,' said Winter, 'let's talk about the list of nicknames. Would you believe that "The Little Prince" is the name of a famous novel written by a French aviator, Antoine de Saint-Exupéry?' The French name rolled off her tongue easily. 'It was about a pilot marooned in the desert.'

Immediately Great-uncle Bartholomew came to mind. But that didn't make any sense at all. If there was one person who *didn't* have the Ormond Riddle and the Jewel, it was him. And surely Rathbone would have known to cross him out, seeing as he was dead.

Winter handed each of us a photocopy of Rathbone's list of nicknames.

'Boges, you said you had something for me,' I said. 'I'm guessing you weren't talking about pies.'

'Hmm, just a sec,' he said with a mouthful. Boges put down his pie, licked his greasy fingers and dived into his school bag again. 'I want you to wear this,' he said, pulling out a small, padded envelope. 'Inside is a failsafe GPS transmitter. You can use it as a distress signal, but they don't come cheap, so it's for emergencies only.'

'In case the Ormond Angel doesn't show up to save me,' I said, opening the package.

'You can put it under the inner sole of your trainer,' said Boges, ignoring my comment, 'under the arch of your foot.' He handed me a pocket knife. 'Here, use this. Cut a small piece of rubber out of your shoe. The transmitter will fit in without creating much of an uncomfortable bump for you to walk on.'

The transmitter was similar to the one Oriana had buried under my skin. I turned it over in my hand.

'Once you activate it, by pressing the tiny switch, it'll set off a distress signal which means I'll be able to track you down.'

I pulled off my left trainer and carefully lifted the inner sole. Where there was a raised part— to support the arch of my foot—I began digging with my knife, cutting out a shape similar to the positioned it against the back wall, we collapsed into it and couldn't stop smiling.'

'Sounds unreal,' said Winter. 'I always wanted a treehouse.'

'We thought it was the coolest treehouse we'd ever seen,' I said. 'Especially after we added a rope ladder and a swing.'

Boges nodded. 'Cal, no-one would even know you're up there—if you're careful—but that doesn't mean you can sit back on that awesome bench and relax, exactly.'

'Boges, I'm always careful and I'm never fully relaxed. That's how I've survived so long. Anyway,' I said, smelling something delicious wafting out of his bag. 'Those pies in your bag aren't going to eat themselves. Get 'em out already!'

Boges pulled out a big paper bag with meat pies inside, while Winter jumped up to fetch some tomato sauce for us from her cupboard.

As we silently ploughed into the food, I tried to remember the last time I'd felt entirely care-free. I had to cast my mind back to way before Dad died. Maybe it was during that last summer we all had together at Treachery Bay. Mum sitting under the beach umbrella with a pile of books, me, Dad and Gab mucking around in the boat. All of us heading into the tiny town for hot chips to go with our catch of the day.

'At Luke Lovett's place,' I added.

'Oh, yeah, I remember,' said Boges, nodding. 'The awesome one we built at the back of his property.'

'That's the one,' I said.

'Aren't you a bit old for cubby houses?' joked Winter.

'These are desperate times,' I said with a shrug.

'Probably not a bad idea, actually,' said Boges. 'It's at least a couple of hundred metres or so from the house, and has great coverage—that's if all those other trees are still surrounding it. And that's if they haven't pulled it down—but why would they? It's a breathtaking example of modern architecture!'

'It was pretty awesome,' I agreed, remembering how hard the three of us had worked to have it finished over one weekend in our school holidays. 'We built it mostly out of wooden panels that we'd collected in wheelbarrows from an old barn that was being torn down nearby,' I explained to Winter. 'We even found this long seat from a train carriage, abandoned by the side of a road, and dragged it back to the tree.'

'Yeah, do you remember how long it took us to get that thing up the tree?' Boges asked me. 'Took us forever to pulley it up—it was so heavy and awkward. But once we got it up there and the results from the Caesar shift programme.'

'And?' I asked.

'Zilch. Nada. Not a single clue. It was all total gibberish.'

I groaned, shaking my head.

'Still,' said Boges, 'you have to look on the bright side.'

'There's a bright side?'

'At least now we know where the Caesar shift *isn't*,' offered Winter.

'Exactly,' agreed Boges.

'Super!' I said, sarcastically. 'So it's been used in the missing last two lines or not at all—that doesn't sound like the bright side to me. We need to start making serious plans. We have to decide on how we're going to get to Ireland, and it looks like we'll have to make do with the help of our copy of the Ormond Riddle and the drawings of the Jewel. In the meantime, I also need another place to live. I just heard on the news that the cops have narrowed my position down to the south-east of the city. I need to get out of here.'

'I can sniff around for something,' said Boges.

'I've already thought of a possible place,' I said. 'Do you remember our treehouse?'

Boges and Winter both looked at me like I was speaking another language.

and answered it, quickly walking away from the inquisitive chemist.

'Cal?'

'Winter, what's up? Are you OK?'

'I'm fine. Just had to get away from Miss Sparks for a moment.' She paused. 'I'm almost done here and Boges is coming straight over after school—the three of us have to get together and plan our next moves—getting the Jewel and the Riddle back, and getting to Ireland. We also need to find out who the three people on that list of nicknames are—one of them will have the goods, I'm sure.'

12 Lesley Street

5:11 pm

'I just had my final physics exam,' said Boges, flopping down at the table with a grin.

'I take it you went well?' said Winter.

'Easy,' he said. 'Too easy for me.'

Winter threw a cushion at him. I picked one up near me and threw it at him too.

'Hey!' he complained, deflecting the cushion attack. 'I'm just being honest! Anyway, you should be happy it's over, because now I have more time to devote my brilliance to the DMO.' He folded his arms. 'And I can also now reveal back. The magpie was still perched there, his sharp eyes following me. All of a sudden I felt like maybe it was my great-uncle watching out for me, reminding me of my need for constant vigilance.

It would be great living high in the treetops, out of sight while quietly keeping watch on the world. When I was a kid, me, Boges and a guy from school called Luke built ourselves a tree-house. Luke lived on a big, bushy block with an incredible climbing tree, right up the back. It had thick, strong branches that formed an ideal platform to build on, and it was in a perfect spot—far away from the house.

I remembered thinking how much I wanted to build one up the back of our house in Richmond—Gabbi would have loved it—but we just didn't have the right tree . . .

1:22 pm

I picked out a cheap hair dye and approached the pharmacy counter.

'Do I know you?' the chemist asked.

'I come in here a bit,' I lied. 'I live around here.'

She nodded as she handed me my change, but didn't once take her eyes off me.

My mobile buzzed in my pocket. I fished it out

'I think I've seen you around here a few times now,' he said. 'Which flat do you live in?'

'I'm just visiting,' I said, trying to keep my answer as vague as possible.

He grunted, clearly unsatisfied, but he nodded as if to say it would do for the moment. I watched as he walked away towards the bus stop further down the street.

I imagined the guy in the suit casually asking the other residents about me, eventually realising that none of them had a sixteen-year-old visiting them. I would have to keep my trips to Winter's flat to a minimum. Or avoid the place altogether.

Something flew at my head as I made my way to the shops. It struck my mirrored sunglasses, startling me, and I ducked, instinctively lifting up an arm to defend myself.

A bird had dive-bombed me from one of the huge fig trees that grew on Winter's street. I looked up, shielding my face, to see the source of the attack. A magpie perched on a low branch in a nearby tree cocked his head and looked at me with serious brown eyes.

I knew it couldn't be Maggers, but as I snatched the mirrored sunglasses off my face I thought of him and my old great-uncle.

As I continued walking to the shops, I looked

It's only a matter of time before we arrest him.'

They weren't bluffing. The south-east of the city was exactly where I was—sitting with my feet up in Winter's flat. It was also the rough location of the St Johns Street house.

I hated admitting it, but I knew I'd have to move on. I decided I'd talk to Winter and Boges when we got together that night, to see if they had any ideas on where I could go. In the mean-time, I'd see what I could do about changing my hair.

I checked myself in the mirror after rubbing a section clear on the misty surface. I'd need to dye my hair again or something. Anything to try and avoid recognition and capture.

I grabbed one of Winter's baseball caps, then put on Boges's mirrored sunglasses, left behind after his Cyril the Sumo act. I'd need to risk a quick trip to the shops to get some more dye. Maybe a darker brown, I thought. Maybe even black.

1:13 pm

No-one was around on the street outside Winter's building, but for some reason I felt exposed.

At the sound of someone coming out of the building behind me, I turned. A man in a suit and black-rimmed glasses gave me a hard look.

2 NOVEMBER

60 days to go . . .

12:00 pm

The muscles in my legs were still sore and tight. Winter was at the library again with her tutor, so I had taken a hot shower then parked myself on the couch with my feet up, next to her radio. I turned up the volume the second I heard my name on the hourly news report.

My stomach started churning when the newsreader mentioned the name 'Senior Sergeant Dorian McGrath'—the guy who'd accused me of kidnapping Gabbi when I was in police custody in the secure wing of Armitage District Hospital.

'The net is closing around Ormond,' said McGrath. 'We have a large, well-equipped intelligence centre which is receiving crucial information about this dangerous young criminal every day. We're building up a strong picture of where he is: We've plotted all of the sightings and have isolated one area—the south-east of the city.

'Sure did,' I said. 'Nearly burst my eardrums, but it gave me enough cover to get away . . . until Ryan took over.'

'Sweet! Sounds like having a double pays off! I have to go, but I have something for you that I'll bring around to Winter's tomorrow afternoon.'

'What is it?' I asked. But Boges had already hung up.

*gone to the library to meet
miss sparks. rest up and i'll
see you later ☺*

winter x

I pulled my phone off its charger and called Boges.

'Boges, it's me. I'm OK.'

'I know,' he said in a hushed voice. 'Winter already called me this morning. Crazy night, huh?'

'Insane!'

'Dude, I'm at school and am about to sit a big exam, so I'll have to go in a sec, but just quickly—I was really worried about the amount of magnesium I used in the Special FX. Did it work?'

him seriously. Otherwise, Rafe, or some other innocent person, could have been taken down by a bullet.

For the time being, at least, the wedding was off. Now I had to return my focus to the real job: locating the Ormond Riddle and the Ormond Jewel and getting them both—together with myself and my friends—to the Keeper of Rare Books at Trinity College in Dublin. And that was only the start of the Ireland investigation.

A long time had passed since that fateful New Year's Eve warning. There were only sixty-one days left in the countdown to December 31st, and in that time we had so much to do. It seemed absolutely impossible. Not only did we have to retrieve the Riddle and the Jewel, and get ourselves over to Ireland, we also had to be the first to put together the clues and uncover the secret of the Ormond Singularity. And find out what really happened to my dad.

Then, of course, there was the matter of clearing my name so that my life on the run could finally come to an end.

We needed to get a serious move on.

10:46 am

The flat was empty but Winter had left a note.

chapel down to Central Station. Then just when I thought I'd run out of chances, Ryan Spencer turned up. It was crazy. We swapped clothes and then he ran off—'

'—and led the chase away so that you could escape,' Winter finished for me. 'It's genius! The perfect decoy! And he can't be arrested, because he's not you!'

'Exactly,' I agreed. 'Although I hope it doesn't come to that—he'd have a lot of explaining to do. I hope he gets away,' I said, noticing that the newsflash had ended and the screen had returned to some late-night fitness infomercial.

4:02 am

I lay awake on the couch, replaying images from last night at Chapel-by-the-Sea. I recalled Gabbi, pulling at the flowers in her hair. I cringed as I pictured Mum and Rafe standing together—about to be wed. I couldn't get my head around it, but I reminded myself that I had succeeded in what I had set out to do. I was there to protect Rafe from the assassin, and that's exactly what I had done.

Next I pictured that weird old fungus guy, Dr Leporello. He'd issued me the warning, for whatever reason, and I was relieved I'd taken to be live footage,' she said. 'I just saw you—a close-up of you, Callum Ormond! How did you get from there to here?'

'I can explain.'

'And what are you wearing?' she frowned, tugging on the check shirt that Ryan had swapped with me. 'You're covered in flecks of white paint, or something.'

'Can I please get a drink first?' I asked as I collapsed in a chair at the table. I ran my hands through my hair, and realised it was full of grit and dirt from the explosions.

Winter looked at me, then back at the screen. 'What's going on? If you're standing right here with me, then who's that on the TV?'

'My ultimate body double,' I said, catching the can she'd tossed to me.

'Ryan? Ryan Spencer? Is that what you're saying? What do you mean? How could that be?'

'Has Boges filled you in on what went down at the chapel?'

'You stopped the hitman and the wedding. Your uncle, mum and Gab are OK; he told me all about it,' she rushed, 'but we had no idea what had happened to you, or whether you got away OK. Please just hurry up and explain *that*,' she said, pointing to the TV once more.

'They chased me for ages, all the way from the

I recalled his November birth date. We didn't share the same birthday and we didn't share the same mum . . . It just wasn't possible.

He'd always run away from me in the past, why had he suddenly decided to help me?

Finally at the top of the stairs, I could see Winter's flat. It wasn't in complete darkness—the flicker of her TV screen was visible, glowing through a window.

I knocked softly at the door.

'Winter, it's me.'

I thought I heard a gasp, and then the volume of the TV was turned down.

'Winter,' I whispered again, 'can you let me in?'

Something tumbled to the floor as her scurrying feet approached. The door opened slowly and her smoky eyes peered through at me.

She looked dazed—maybe she'd been asleep on the couch. Slowly she stepped back and let me pass, all the time staring at me like I was a ghost.

'But how can you be here,' she murmured, 'when you're also over there?'

I glanced over to where she was pointing. On the TV screen, a grainy, shaky aerial image showed Ryan's figure, circled by chopper light, running along the Georges River.

She looked at me for an answer. 'It's meant

the helicopter was sweeping over the cityscape, just beyond the station. I waited about ten minutes before silently making my way towards the basketball courts and hauling myself up the perimeter fence.

From my vantage point, high up the wire netting, I could just make out Ryan in the distance, a running silhouette in my clothes, circled in the chopper spotlight, leading the chase far, far away from the 'real' me.

The drone of the fugitive chase was fading with every metre that Ryan led the fierce hunt away. Around me, the sounds of the night had almost returned to normal. I hung from the netting like an exhausted monkey, before finally releasing my grip and letting myself drop to the ground.

12 Lesley Street

3:20 am

I plodded up the stairs to Winter's flat, climbing like I was about a hundred years old. I owed Ryan Spencer big time. He'd shown up like a decoy clone, saved my exhausted butt, and left me behind with my mind spinning.

We were so similar, he *had* to be my twin, but nothing made sense. What had happened to us?

me a cap to wear. 'Anyway, if they do catch me, they can't arrest *me*, can they—I mean, I'm not you, am I?!'

Stunned, I buttoned up the shirt he'd given me to wear. He pulled my blazer's collar up around his face.

'Wish me luck,' he grinned, only his sunburnt nose showing. 'I'll take them on for as long as possible. I won my school's under-15 cross-country race last year, so I should be able to give you plenty of time to get away.'

I was about to tell him that I'd won *my* school's under-15 cross-country race last year too, when he stepped out of the alcove, nodded to me, turned and ran.

The sound of his footsteps soon disappeared, and then the sirens picked up their wailing again, clearly having spotted Ryan—posing as me—emerging from the station.

I sank into the alcove as the SWAT team, chasing Ryan on foot, ran right past me and my hiding spot. I held my breath as they thundered by, intent on capturing the lone figure in the blazer ahead of them.

The identity switch had worked!

1:28 am

Carefully I peered out. The brilliant beam from

Before saying another word, Ryan dragged me around a corner and into a little alcove. My heaving body and straining lungs were at the point of collapse. I could barely defend myself.

'Take a breather. The helicopter can't see you in here.'

'You're really trying to help me?' I gasped, doubled over. There were so many other questions I wanted to ask him, but now wasn't the time.

'That's right,' he said. 'Beats a night of tagging. And it's not like I can keep on tagging when the entire police force has descended on the city. That would be asking for trouble.'

'So do you know somewhere we can hide?'

'I have a better idea. Nothing beats a good relay race, Cal.'

'A relay race?'

'Pass the baton, bro!'

Before I could even comprehend what he was saying, he grabbed at my blazer, wrenching it from me, while shrugging off his check shirt.

'Quick, let's swap,' he said, as he began pulling on my blazer, over a singlet. 'I'll continue the chase for you. Put my shirt on and stay here. We don't have much time.'

'But if they catch you—' I started to say.

'Don't worry; they're not going to catch me. Not if I can help it. Come on,' he urged, passing strides away. I would have to fight him with whatever strength I had left.

'Cal!' he shouted. 'Stop running! It's me!'

The voice was familiar, but I wasn't sure why.

'Cal, it's just me!'

Finally I stopped and stared, clenching my fists.

I couldn't believe my eyes.

'Ryan?' I croaked.

Ryan Spencer pounded up to me. The face I knew so well was staring at me, grinning. 'You're so fast—I thought I'd never catch up with you,' he said between puffs. 'I saw the whole thing on the news on my mobile. Recognised where you were and thought maybe I should help for once, instead of running away from you.'

I was stunned to hear my voice coming out of this guy's mouth like echoing feedback on a long-distance call. Looking at his face was like looking at a painting of me—except for a few small details that the artist hadn't quite perfected.

Why would he want to help me all of a sudden? I turned to start running again—I couldn't trust him, and I had to keep moving—but just as I was about to charge away, he grabbed me.

'Get off me! Let me go!'

'Calm down! I'm trying to help you!'

'I have to get away before the cops catch me!'

pain but I forced them on. I gritted my teeth and silently begged for a way to throw the cops off my tail. I had to cheat the man-hunt.

1:12 am

I hurtled past the basketball courts and pound-ed up the ramp towards the station entrance. Startled late commuters jumped out of my way—they must have seen the crazed determination in my eyes.

The helicopters couldn't chase me undercover, but I could hear pounding feet close behind me.

Someone was right behind me—running heaps harder than I was.

Out of the corner of my eye I could see the figure gaining on me. It was just one guy chasing me on foot.

Was it a cop? He wasn't in uniform. A plain-clothes cop?

If I couldn't get away from him and lose myself somewhere in the station, I was done for.

Every step was agony as my exhausted body demanded rest, but the cop behind me was almost on top of me, yelling out my name.

Desperate, I looked around for somewhere to jump to, dive into—anything to get this guy off my back. I threw another quick glance behind me—he was about my size and he was just a few to do. There was no way I could hide out in a shed or back garden, but I was tiring with every step. A house-to-house search would eventually find me, no matter how carefully I'd chosen my refuge. My only alternative was to keep moving—fast.

I bolted away, heading for a long sloping road that was crammed on both sides with old terraced houses. It was harder here for the helicopter to see me, because I could duck under awnings and into side streets. But none of that could fool the ground forces.

12:51 am

The sirens were getting closer and I knew I couldn't keep this up. Every time I thought I'd outwitted the police helicopter, it would reappear a moment later, rising in the night sky behind me or, scarier still, up ahead.

Right now it hovered almost on top of me, swinging towards me with its probing light. The deafening wind-rush from its rotors was flattening the grass and whipping my hair. Cop cars skidded and screeched in from all directions.

I zigzagged left and right, scanning my surroundings for an escape route.

By now I recognised where I was—approaching Central Station. My muscles screamed with veins. I launched myself over the side gate and into the front yard. I flew down the driveway and into the street, crossing it in three huge strides.

Straight down the side of another house, I ran through an open gate and out again, then continued past the backyard barbecue and over the rear fence. On the other side I found myself at the start of an open field—not a good place for someone on the run. A fast-moving body was way too obvious in this still and empty space.

Sticking to the fence line, I ran around the edge of the houses that backed onto the field. The cover of darkness wasn't enough to hide me here, so I knew it wouldn't be long before I was spotted again.

Within minutes, the choppers were hovering over my head, and from somewhere the sirens were approaching.

I spotted a gap in someone's fence and squeezed through it, tearing my clothes on rusty nails in the process. I ran across the yard, around the side of the house and straight out onto another road.

The staccato beat of the choppers in the sky constantly thumped in my head, forcing me to keep going.

But I couldn't throw them. I didn't know what

The spotlight from the chopper above had returned and was skimming around me, still yet to lock onto my position. The sound of another helicopter approached, completely freaking me out. I looked up and could just make out the TV news logo on the side. The media had finally shown up. They were like vultures in the sky, waiting for their opportunity to pounce on some helpless, withering creature.

I wasn't about to let that creature be me.

I jumped over a fence and tumbled into some-one's backyard. I scrambled to my feet, took one step and almost crash-dived into a swimming pool! I leaped to the right and raced up the side of the house, tripping and almost falling as my foot got stuck in the loop of a garden hose. I barely managed to keep my balance as I grabbed hold of a tree branch reaching over the fence.

I was gripping the rough bark of the branch to steady myself when the whole tree started to shake! A roar of squeals shattered the night air and a swarm of black, flapping wings streaked around and over me!

Bats! A whole leathery colony of them! I'd disturbed their midnight feasting. I jumped back and covered my face.

They screeched off into the sky as I ducked and kept going. Adrenaline pumped into my flashing lights from the police cars that had earlier screeched to a standstill behind me strobed through the lingering smoke, pulsing out a murky blue and orange beat.

'Spread out! He can't have gone far!' a voice screamed out from only metres away. My ears were still ringing, but I'd heard those frightening orders loud and clear.

I dropped to my hands and knees and began crawling, praying that the low smoke would hide me long enough to put some distance between me and my pursuers. I followed the roadside kerbing which turned right, sharply.

As I clambered further away from the main street, my cover was thinning. A quick glance behind me showed the grey clouds from the Special FX lifting and dissolving. A cluster of dim lights were beginning to fan out—proof of police on foot.

'There he is!' another voice shouted. 'Down there! He's about to turn down that lane! Don't lose him!'

The beams of light grew stronger, criss-crossing through the darkness, searching for me. I stood up and I sprinted down the lane, the sounds of thudding boots storming close by. I'd completely broken out of the smoke now and only had the dark to hide me.

as they struggled on the ground, shocked and blinded by the brilliant flash.

Seconds later, a rain of stones and soil drummed down from the sky. I ducked and covered my head with my hands. My ears were still ringing and my sight was blurry but one thing was clear to me—it worked! The Special FX had taken its sweet time, but it had worked!

12:06 am

The dazzling flare slowly subsided, leaving behind columns of billowing smoke in the night air. I had to shut my mouth and eyes against the dirt and dust. In the confusion, the disoriented cops tripped and stumbled over, swearing at each other—and me—as they collided.

I squinted up to try and locate the helicopter. A greyish glow was haphazardly sweeping over the area. Its powerful light had been eclipsed by black smoke and dust—they'd completely lost my position. There was no way I was going to let them locate me now. This was my chance.

Blindly, I split off sideways and away from the haze of scrambling bodies on the street. Stumbling across the footpath, I groped my way along, almost colliding with a couple of thick tree trunks.

I blinked and rubbed my stinging eyes as my vision slowly started straightening out. The

1 NOVEMBER

61 days to go . . .

12:00 am

The cops closed in on me, carefully advancing in two arcs—the classic pincer movement. I couldn't believe my desperate dash from the chapel—after stopping the hitman from shooting Rafe—had ended up here. Far away from where it all began, but surrounded.

I was panting, breathlessly staring down at the motionless Special FX canister that was gleaming in the moonlight. I willed it to do something—anything!

Did it move? I thought I saw it shimmer, but wasn't sure.

A blinding wall of white flame suddenly erupted from the road, shooting up an impenetrable barrier! I was floored. The sound of the explosion almost burst my eardrums!

As I crawled to my feet, I could hear the muffled screams of the cops and SWAT guys surrounded. I throw the canister of Special FX—Boges's latest creation—in a last-chance effort to escape. But it's a dud. It doesn't go off. I'm done for.

Oriana and Sligo argue over the Ormond Riddle and Jewel, making it clear that neither of them have the goods. Sligo discovers that the room is bugged and the party quickly disperses.

25 OCTOBER
A search through Rathbone's office reveals a secret drawer with heaps of information on the Ormond family. I also find a file belonging to Charles G Fong—Winter's dad. This file finally proves to Winter that her parents didn't disinherit her after all, and that Sligo forged her father's will.

Boges reluctantly gives me the startling news that my mum and Rafe are getting married on 31 October. Dr Leporello informs me that a contract killer will make an attempt on Rafe during the ceremony.

31 OCTOBER
I arrive at the chapel early and hide in the loft next to the organ. As the ceremony proceeds, a man with a weapon steps out from the shadows. I race down the stairs and throw Boges's Disappearing Dust. People are running, screaming, from the chapel. I hope I have halted the killer.

I flee as fast as I can, but I'm quickly pursued by cops with the aid of a chopper. Soon I'm

The plan is going smoothly until the real Oriana and Sumo show up! Winter and Boges, with the contents of the safety deposit box in their possession, just make it out of the door in time.

Later we discover that the contents of the box are fakes! Someone else has the real Jewel and Riddle! But who?

23 OCTOBER

Rafe, Mum and Gabbi have gone away to Treachery Bay, so Boges and I take the opportunity to search their house. I find a couple of interesting things but most bizarre of all I realise that my mum's personal things are in Rafe's room. They've become much closer than I had hoped. I don't want to think about it.

24 OCTOBER

Sligo is preparing a banquet where he intends to establish a connection between himself and Oriana de la Force. Winter agrees to co-host the event with him to keep him on her side and to see if she can gather any more information about the DMO.

With the help of a spycam in Winter's necklace, Boges and I watch the banquet unfold while hidden in Sligo's pool shed. Among the dinner guests, we spot Rathbone and Murray 'Toecutter' Durham.

about his money laundering. Boges, Winter and I arrive early to prepare for the meeting. After Rathbone hands over the will, he tries to convince me to disappear and change my identity.

14 OCTOBER
Piers Ormond's will reveals that if the Ormond Singularity isn't claimed by its rightful owner before 31 December, this year, it will revert to the Crown.

17 OCTOBER
A chance encounter with Repro leads me to his new place—the cavern. After we spend half the night transporting his belongings over an underground lake, Repro notices the writing on my ankle that appeared after I was dumped in Dingo Bones Valley. He tells me it's a safety deposit box number. Oriana's PIN!

20 OCTOBER
Winter and Boges prepare their Oriana and Sumo disguises and we finalise the last details of the bank heist.

21 OCTOBER
In costume, and carrying the fake fingerprint, Winter and Boges confidently enter Zürich Bank.

advice on blackmail. He suggests a surveillance operation.

A metal trader gives me six hundred dollars for half of my gold stash.

8 OCTOBER
Oriana de la Force has been charged with Gabbi's kidnapping. Winter thinks Kelvin must have dobbed her in. Boges obtains Rathbone's home address, so we begin surveillance.

11 OCTOBER
Winter and I catch Rathbone at a suspicious dinner meeting where suitcases are exchanged. We follow him back to his house and watch in amazement as he digs up a wooden box in his backyard. He proceeds to transfer thousands of dollars from the suitcase into it. Winter and I both snap photos of him in the act, then flee.

12 OCTOBER
Boges anonymously emails one of the incriminating photos to Rathbone.

13 OCTOBER
I call Rathbone and tell him to come to Crookwood Cemetery where he must hand over Piers Ormond's will in exchange for my discretion

1 OCTOBER

The old prospectors and their vicious dog, Sniffer, are gaining on me. I plunge into a thorny bush, hoping the dog will avoid it. I'm stunned when he charges towards me, only to lick my face before running off and leading my would-be captors away from me.

Back in the city I call Boges and find out that Winter managed to keep hold of the bag with Oriana's fingerprint on it. Our plans to infiltrate Zürich Bank to recover the Ormond Jewel and Riddle are progressing.

2 OCTOBER

Boges is busy working on perfecting Oriana's fingerprint, so we can fool the bank scanner. All we need now is her PIN.

4 OCTOBER

Sheldrake Rathbone has Piers Ormond's will, and I want it from him. I speak to Nelson Sharkey for

To Milly and Charlie

Note: This story is set in Australia, where November is a spring month

First published by Scholastic Australia Pty Ltd in 2010
First published in Great Britain in 2010 by Hodder Children's Books,
under licence from Scholastic Australia Pty Ltd

A Catalogue record for this book is available from the British
Library

ISBN 978 0 340 99654 6

Printed and bound by CPI Bookmarque Ltd, Croydon, Surrey

The paper and board used in this paperback by Hodder Children's
Books are natural recyclable products made from wood grown in
sustainable forests. The manufacturing processes conform to the
environmental regulations of the country of origin.

Hodder Children's Books
A division of Hachette Children's Books
338 Euston Road, London NW1 3BH
An Hachette UK company
www.hachette.co.uk

CONSPIRACY 365

BOOK ELEVEN: NOVEMBER

GABRIELLE LORD

*Hodder
Children's
Books*

A division of Hachette Children's Books